K.

6/07

Mulch Ado About Nothing

**Center Point
Large Print**

**This Large Print Book carries the
Seal of Approval of N.A.V.H.**

Mulch Ado About Nothing

JILL CHURCHILL

CENTER POINT PUBLISHING
THORNDIKE, MAINE

This Center Point Large Print edition
is published in the year 2006 by arrangement with
William Morrow, a division of HarperCollins Publishers.

The text of this Large Print edition is unabridged. In other
aspects, this book may vary from the original edition. Printed in
Thailand. Set in 16-point Times New Roman type.

ISBN 1-58547-741-9

Library of Congress Cataloging-in-Publication Data

Churchill, Jill, 1943-
    Mulch ado about nothing / Jill Churchill.--Center Point large print ed.
        p. cm.
    ISBN 1-58547-741-9 (lib. bdg. : alk. paper)
    1. Jeffry, Jane (Fictitious character)--Fiction. 2. Women detectives--Illinois--
Chicago--Fiction. 3. Gardening--Fiction. 4. Single mothers--Fiction. 5. Chicago
(Ill.)--Fiction. 6. Large type books. I. Title.

PS3553.H85M85 2006
813'.54--dc22

                                                                2005028476

Mulch Ado About Nothing

One

Note on Jane Jeffry's kitchen door:

Jane, you got flowers but you weren't home. I've got them. They're beautiful! Where are you?

Shelley

Note on Shelley Nowack's kitchen door:

Shelley, just phoning in my summer PTA excuse. Couldn't hang up to answer the door when I was begging off. I <u>want</u> my flowers.

Jane

Note on Jane's kitchen door:

Just ran to drop off a couple books before the library police send out a squad car for them. What's the occasion for the flowers? I wouldn't *dream* of opening the card, of course.

Shelley

Note on Shelley's door:

Had to drive to Jenny's house to give Katie lunch money. What kind of flowers? And don't you dare open the card!

Jane

Note on Jane's door:

Sorry, I wasn't gone. I was washing the dog after he got loose and rolled in something revolting. I want to know why you're getting flowers.

Shelley

Note on Shelley's door:

I want to know, too. I've got to make a smash and grab at the grocery store or we'll have stale bread and crystallized jelly for dinner. Mike's getting cranky about having so much mac and cheese.

Jane

Note on Jane's door:

I haven't opened the note yet. But I've held it up to a strong light and the envelope is too thick to read through. I'm following you to the grocery store.

Shelley

Note on Shelley's door:

Didn't you hear me honking at you in the parking lot? If you didn't drive twice the speed limit, I'd have caught up with you. So I came home and you aren't here. Do you have flower preservatives? They're going to need it if I'm ever going to see them. I'm going to sit in a lawn chair in my driveway until you get home.

Jane

Jane didn't do quite what she'd threatened, but she settled in to read the paper on the top step of her kitchen-door deck. When Shelley's minivan turned in—not quite on two wheels, but almost—Jane flung down the paper. "Where are my flowers?" she demanded.

"In the kitchen," Shelley said. "I'll fetch them for you. What are they for? Who are they from? What have you done to deserve flowers that I don't know about?"

"I have no idea," Jane said. She hoisted herself up, grimacing at a twinge in her knee, and went into her house, leaving the door open for Shelley, who reappeared a moment later, almost concealed by a huge flower arrangement.

"Oh, they *are* beautiful!" she exclaimed as Shelley set them on the kitchen table.

"Read the card," Shelley said, shoving it at Jane. The card looked a bit worn and was scorched on one corner. Jane started laughing. "What's so funny?" Shelley demanded.

"What a spy you'd make! You spent the day trying to find out what the message was and didn't read the envelope. The flowers are for Julie Jackson, that stylish woman who lives at the same number address as mine, but two blocks west. You know, the one who's

9

doing that garden class we're starting on Monday."

They looked at each other for a long moment, then Jane said, "Have you tried steaming the envelope open?"

Their "better selves" prevailed and they didn't steam open the envelope, but instead Shelley drove to Julie Jackson's house with Jane clutching the flower arrangement and sniffing the heady odor of the white lilies in it.

Shelley said, "You've got pollen from the lilies all over your face. You look jaundiced."

Jane tried hanging on to the arrangement with one hand while hastily brushing her face off. "Better?" she asked, looking at her hands, which were bright orange with pollen.

Shelley had just turned the corner on the street they needed and slowed almost to a stop. "Jane, look."

"Look? I can't even see around these flowers. What?"

"There's a police tape around Julie Jackson's yard. And three police cars and an ambulance."

"Oh, no!"

Shelley pulled over to the side of the street one house away. Jane got out and set the flower arrangement on the grass and dragged a tissue out of her pocket to wipe more pollen off her face. Two people came out of the house Jane and Shelley had been heading for. A woman who looked like Julie Jackson and a man who was a head taller than she and wearing a suit that looked too hot for such a warm day.

A uniformed police officer was following them, almost herding them out of the house.

"Rats!" Jane said. "I just caught a glimpse of Mel inside that window by the door. What do you suppose is going on? And who are that couple?"

Shelley, having no more information than Jane, said nothing. They just stood there, transfixed and wondering what to do with the huge flower arrangement.

Detective Mel VanDyne had spotted Jane as well, and came out the front door a moment later. Scowling fiercely, he had a brief word with the unknown couple and the officer with them and turned and headed toward Jane and Shelley.

"What are you two doing here?" he snapped. "Gawking?"

He should have known from the sizzling silence that met this inquiry that he was going to be sorry for that remark. But he compounded the looming problem by adding in an unfortunately demanding tone, "Well?"

Jane said coldly, "I don't normally carry around a huge vase of florist flowers when I'm just out for a 'gawk.' Perhaps you've noticed that about me over the years? These flowers," she said, pointing at the arrangement, "were delivered to me by mistake and were meant for Julie Jackson. Shelley and I were merely bringing them to her."

Shelley was about to butt in, but thought better of it. Jane was doing fine by herself. She picked up the flower arrangement and handed it to Mel.

He was trying to figure out how to apologize without actually saying the word "sorry" and feeling very stupid holding a vast arrangement of flowers at the crime scene. In a more pleasant voice, he said, "I see."

"They're probably evidence," Jane said, turning on her heel dramatically to get back into the car. She tripped over the curb and came down hard on her right foot, and her shoe turned sideways with a sickening popping noise that made her yelp involuntarily.

Mel set down the flowers, and he and Shelley rushed to scoop her up.

"Are you okay?" Mel asked.

"Aside from ruining my exit, I think so," Jane said, grimacing with pain. "I'm feeling a tad faint."

Mel opened the car door, shoved her into the passenger seat, and made her take off her shoe and felt her foot. "No obvious break. Can you move your ankle?"

Jane felt like crying, not only because her foot was hurting horribly, but because she'd made a bit of a fool of herself by flouncing off like that. She wiggled it around and said, "My ankle's fine. Just leave me alone."

To her dismay, Mel and Shelley took her at her word. Jane put her shoe back on, muttering to herself, "Stupid, stupid, stupid."

Mel looked at the flower arrangement sitting unevenly on the grass. "Who are the flowers from?"

Shelley shrugged. "We don't know. The envelope is sealed."

He pulled out the little clear plastic stake and glanced

at the card. "Why's it scorched?"

"How would I know?" Shelley said airily.

Mel held the envelope by one corner, slit it open with a penknife, pulled out the card with a pair of tweezers, and glanced at it. "Hmm."

Shelley craned her neck to see what the card said. There was no signature.

"What does it say?" Jane asked from inside Shelley's van.

"It says, 'You're next,'" Shelley reported. "No name. Jane, you need to go home and get some ice on your foot to keep it from bruising." Shelley walked around the front of the van and got in.

Mel came to Jane's window. "I'm sorry," he admitted.

"So am I," Jane said, but her words drifted on the wind as Shelley took off like a rocket.

"So what do you think happened?" Shelley asked when she'd helped Jane up the steps, into her house, and onto the sofa.

"Something awful for sure. I'm still mad at Mel for accusing us of going over there to 'gawk.' There I am, with about three tons of lilies and baby's breath in my arms, and he thinks we just horned in to take a looky-loo."

Shelley went to Jane's refrigerator, found ice, a plastic bag, and a dish towel. She was putting together an ice pack while saying, "There wasn't a body brought out. That must mean that somebody was just hurt and was being treated. I hope."

"Or that they were waiting for the photographers before moving the body."

"Don't be depressing," Shelley said.

"I am depressed. My foot really hurts again. It was kind of numb for a while, but . . ."

"Take off your shoe and put it up on the sofa."

Wincing, Jane removed her sneaker. The foot was red and swollen and had an imprint of everything on the inside of the shoe on her skin. A deep purple mark was along the outside of her foot.

"Jane, that doesn't look good."

"Just give me an hour with the ice bag. It'll be okay."

"Not if you've broken something."

"I didn't fall that hard. Really. I have iron bones. I've never broken one before."

Shelley sighed with exasperation. "You're going to have to get an X ray. And there's no point in even arguing with me. I'll haul you bodily from that sofa if I have to."

Jane knew Shelley meant it. She tried to put her shoe back on, but her foot, in mere minutes, had swollen so much she couldn't cram her foot in.

Four hours later they returned home. Two hours had been spent waiting in the emergency room of the local hospital where most of the other patients were elderly people who seemed to regard it as a community gathering place and called cheerfully to one another. One hour had been spent waiting in a room that looked like a prison cell for the X ray to come back, and another hour for the orthopedist to explain Jane had broken the long bone at the outside of her foot and truss her up in a toes-to-knee cast. Then they had to stop at a pharmacy so Shelley could go in and buy crutches.

"They would have given me crutches at the hospital," Jane said.

"And charged your insurance about a thousand dollars. I know where to buy a pair for thirty-five dollars."

"How do you happen to know that?" Jane said, staring down at her leg.

"Had to provide some for a school play once. The kids played with them until they were in splinters. That was in the old days when they were made of wood. Remember? Your Katie and my Denise spent half of one summer seeing how far they could fling themselves by putting them way out in front and swinging forward. Here we are. I'll come around to help you. Stay right where you are."

Jane managed to bash her other leg twice with the crutches just getting out of the car when they got home.

"Don't hang on them by your armpits, Jane. Hold the handle and barely touch the bad foot to the ground while you bring the good one forward."

"I wish you'd let me at least shave my leg before we went. Think how hairy it'll be by the time this is taken off." She tried to follow Shelley's instructions and lost one of the crutches, which went spinning off down the driveway.

Shelley picked it up and patiently handed it back.

"Now, with the steps—"

Jane interrupted. "I'm not doing steps. I'm going up backwards on my butt."

"For several weeks?" Shelley asked.

"If need be." Jane hobbled to the bottom of the three steps up to her deck outside the kitchen and demonstrated how well she could haul herself backwards.

"I hope you don't have any social engagements coming up where there are stairs," Shelley commented.

"Social engagements? No. I'm going to take every advantage of this and lie about looking wan and frail and ask people to bring me ginger ale and Cheez-its at regular intervals."

TWO

"You did call Katie and Mike, didn't you?" Jane asked when she was installed on the sofa in the living room.

"All you have is Wheat Thins. No Cheez-its. Want wine or soda?" Shelley called from the kitchen. "And yes, I called your kids. Told them not to worry. I didn't call the soccer camp where Todd is, though, because you didn't have the number with you."

"How could you tell them not to worry about me?"

"You want them to worry?"

"It's their turn," Jane said. "I've been the sole worrier in this house for twenty-one years."

Shelley brought in a plate of crackers and cheese and

a soft drink. Somewhere she'd actually found a nice little silver tray and a doily. "Where on earth did you find *that?*" Jane asked, astonished.

"In that cabinet over your refrigerator. Left over from some party or another."

"There's a cabinet over my refrigerator? I'd forgotten."

"Get your mind off the kitchen. How can we find out what happened to Julie Jackson?" Shelley said, sitting down in a chair next to the sofa.

"I've been so obsessed with myself," Jane admitted, "that I've hardly thought about her. I hope she isn't dead or even seriously hurt."

"It looked serious to me. They don't put up crime tapes when somebody tumbles off a step stool."

"I was looking forward to the botany class starting Monday," Jane said. "I hope this was all a misunderstanding and she'll still be teaching it. I met her at a city council meeting once when the cat-haters were yapping about laws to keep cats on leashes. She had some pretty sharp things to say about the balance of nature and I liked her a lot. That woman coming out of the house looked like her. Wonder if it's a sister."

The kitchen door opened and Jane's eldest child, Mike, came in. "Wow! A cast and crutches and everything. Cool! Does it hurt?"

"Does it hurt? Of course it hurts!" She paused. "But not a whole lot," she admitted. "The problem is the crutches. I can't control them."

"Let me try," Mike said delightedly.

Since he was about a foot taller than his mother, he had to hunch over like an old man to even reach the handles, but managed to lurch around the room briskly.

"So how are you going to decorate the cast?" he asked, tossing the crutches back on the sofa and lowering himself to the floor with the grace that only twenty-year-old knees can manage. "Shame it's a plain white one. The stuff they wrap it with these days comes in neon colors and with sports emblems, you know. Scott had one for a while on his hand in magenta."

"Neither sports emblems nor magenta goes with my wardrobe," Jane said. "Besides, I wasn't offered another color."

The doorbell rang and Mike went to let Mel in. "Anything you want fetched, Mom?" Mike asked when he was halfway up the steps to his room.

"Carryout dinner," Jane replied.

Mel had seated himself in the other chair next to the sofa. "Bad break?" he asked sympathetically.

"Just a fracture in a big bone," Jane replied. "I saw the X ray. I never knew there were so many bones in a foot. What happened to Julie Jackson?"

Mel sighed. "She's alive at least. In a coma. She was attacked in her basement, which is a sort of workshop. Lots of lights over seedlings and a desk, computer, and a whole lot of file drawers. Apparently she hit her head on the corner of one that was open as she fell. She was certainly a well-organized person. Each file was labeled, and the contents in one of those paper folders with the clips."

"That's obsessive," Jane commented.

Shelley bridled. "No, it's not. I do that. Haven't you ever reached into a file and thought you pulled everything out, but left behind a small paper that fell out of the bunch?"

Jane didn't dare comment on Shelley's remark. Shelley herself was pretty obsessive. Instead, she asked Mel, "How do you know she was attacked? Maybe she just tripped and fell."

"Signs of a struggle," Mel said shortly. "Short and violent, as if the attacker was as surprised as she was."

"How did he—or she—get in the house?" Shelley asked.

"The back door was unlocked. Just like both of yours probably are."

Jane and Shelley exchanged guilty glances.

"You said the attacker was probably surprised," Jane said. "How do you know that?"

"I don't know for sure. I'm speculating. Her sister and the sister's husband are staying with her and left the house this morning to go into Chicago. The sister looks a lot like Ms. Jackson. If someone were watching for the house to be empty, he might have thought it was Ms. Jackson leaving with a man."

"Was it just a burglary then?"

"Maybe it was intended to be, but there was no sign of anything missing from the rest of the house and she has a nice collection of expensive, hockable little things in open cabinets. The desk in the basement was messed up, papers strewn every which way, but that might have been a result of a struggle."

"Maybe the burglar got too scared to start his work," Shelley said.

"But who would go to the basement before scooping up the good stuff on the ground floor?" Jane asked.

"Exactly," Mel replied, helping himself to some of Jane's crackers and cheese.

Before they could ask what he meant by that, he added, "I have a man coming to fingerprint the two of you."

"Why us?" Shelley asked indignantly.

"Elimination. The envelope on the flower arrangement is covered with prints. I suspect they all belong to you and the proprietor of the flower shop. But the person who sent them might have handled the envelope as well. And we still have to figure out the scorch marks."

Shelley sighed loudly and owned up. "I did that. I'd misread the name on the envelope and thought they were for Jane since they were delivered to her house. When I couldn't catch up with her, I tried to read the note by putting the envelope on a lightbulb."

"Now you tell me!"

"Mel, do you think that flower delivery had something to do with the crime?" Jane asked.

"I've no idea. But the message was cryptic and could be a threat. 'You're next' sounds ominous. Especially as it isn't signed."

20

"You must have checked with the florist," Shelley said, trying to ask the question tactfully.

It wasn't tactful enough. "Of course," Mel said irritably. "He was swamped with orders for a funeral of some big-deal politician. A man came in and paid cash for the flowers and delivery. Nobody remembers what he looked like. No, that's not quite true. The florist, the clerk, and a witness all *think* they know his appearance and entirely disagree."

"But it was a man," Shelley said.

Mel grinned. "According to the clerk, it could have been a woman dressed like a man. He's young and has a vivid imagination."

"Get back to Julie. Do the doctors think she's seriously hurt?" Jane said, glancing down at her cast. She had things medical on her mind. She could have broken her leg, not just a bone in her foot.

"Anybody who's in a coma is in serious trouble," Mel said. "The sister's husband is with her. He's a neurologist and they were here visiting while he attended some sort of convention in the city."

"And the sister?"

"Geneva Jackson," Mel said. "Kept her own last name. She's in some kind of business related to Julie Jackson's, which I haven't quite figured out yet. The sister says Julie was a microbiologist, whatever that is, and reeled off a long list of academic credits. Apparently Julie Jackson had a doctorate."

"She was listed that way in the brochure. Dr. Julie Jackson," Jane said.

"What brochure?"

"The township and the junior college got some kind of grant to get speakers throughout the summer," Shelley explained. "Adult education classes in everything from weight loss to botany and accounting. The first ten people to sign up for each class get to take them for free. Jane and I are enthusiastic but not very knowledgeable gardeners, so we signed up for that one."

"And Ms. Jackson was to be the speaker?"

" 'Group leader,' they called it," Shelley said with a sneer. "What's wrong with 'teacher,' anyway? If we all knew as much as she presumably does, we wouldn't be going. Teachers teach. At least they didn't call her a 'facilitator.' That was all the rage for a while. So stupid."

Since this was obvious and one of Shelley's frequent rants, neither Mel nor Jane replied. A long silence fell and Mel finally stirred first. "I've got to get back to work. Jane, are Mike or Katie going to be around to help you?"

"I'm around," Shelley said, "and I'll help her, but only as much as she actually needs."

"That sounds like a threat," Jane said.

"It is. And the first thing I'm going to help you with is learning to use the crutches so you can't lollygag around being utterly helpless. You'd put on five pounds at least."

Mel slipped away while they bickered.

Three

By Sunday morning, Jane had given up trying to influence the crutches. She was better off, she decided, using only one and having her left hand free to grab things when she lost her balance. This technique also allowed her to carry small objects, which she hadn't been able to with both hands wrestling with crutches. On Sunday afternoon Shelley bought her a pair of knee-length shorts that had lots of big pockets.

"Shelley, the last thing I need is pockets on my thighs. They already bulge and I'd look like one of those misshapen bodybuilders with the monster thighs if I put anything in the pockets."

"Okay by me, but where are you going to carry all the stuff that's normally in your purse when you go out?"

Jane thought a moment. "I could get a purse with a long strap and sling it over my shoulder."

"And have it flap around every time you lurch?"

"It's not me lurching. It's the crutches. The crutches have a mind of their own. I can't tell you how many times they've turned me left when I want to go straight ahead. Even one of them does that to me."

"Then just keep turning left and you'll eventually be facing the right way," Shelley said with a wicked laugh. "Anything you need?"

"A Sherpa," Jane said. "To fetch and carry for me. I keep dropping things and have to put the crutches down to pick the things up, then bend down and pick the crutches back up and usually drop the first thing again. Remember that movie we saw, *Quest for Fire*, and the Neanderthal who was trying to pick up all the melons at the same time and kept dropping them? I feel like that guy."

Early Monday morning, Shelley called on the phone. "Are we going to the botany class?"

"I assumed it wasn't happening," Jane said. "Mel told me Julie Jackson's still in a coma."

"But they might have scrambled and got a replacement teacher," Shelley said. "Let's run down to the community center and see."

Jane had spent most of the weekend on the sofa, knocking back soft drinks and snacks. She'd weigh a ton if she kept that up. "You'll drive, or should I?"

"Have you checked your car insurance?" Shelley asked.

"My car insurance?"

"I'm told most insurance companies won't pay for an accident if the driver has a cast on the right foot."

"Are you really telling me I can't take myself anywhere at all? For weeks! I'll go mad!"

"Be ready in about ten minutes," Shelley said.

"My cast is wet."

"Oh? Will that slow you down?"

"No, I'm just complaining. I put a plastic bag around it like you said to do before showering. Taped it up with masking tape that turned out not to be waterproof.

24

When we go out, could we stop and let me get something better to tape it with?"

Jane was waiting in the driveway in eight minutes. She'd experimented with an old purse with a long strap, and Shelley was right that it flapped around and unbalanced her. The pockets of the baggy, much-pocketed shorts Shelley had bought her were full. Checkbook, ballpoint pen, notepad, lipstick, billfold, a box of tissues, house keys, a bag of lemon drops in case she suddenly felt weak with hunger.

"You do look a bit like the Michelin Man," Shelley said, opening the car door for her. "Watch it. You just cracked my shin with that crutch. Want a boost? That step into the van is high."

"Sorry," Jane said. "Everybody in my house is afraid of me. Especially Willard the Cowardly Dog and the cats." She fumbled around for the seat belt to drag herself up. "I've accidently smacked all of them a couple times when they got underfoot, and Willard got goosed when he stepped in front of me. I think they've decided crutches are some sort of threshing machine and will never come near me again. Max and Meow still sleep at the foot of my bed, but when I get up to go to the bathroom at night, they scatter for shelter."

There were quite a few cars parked at the community center and a large bus getting ready to haul off the twenty adults who were taking a Zoo Maintenance course. A truck from a craft store was unloading some rented sewing machines and sergers for another class that was being held in the building. And a number of women wearing remarkably unflattering gymnastic clothes were waiting for their ride to an aerobic dancing studio.

"If I ever dress like that, have me locked up," Jane said.

Shelley looked her up and down. "You're hardly better today. You're quite lumpy. Are you packed for a three-day camp-out?"

"Just the everyday necessities. Oh, no. I'd forgotten there were stairs."

"There's a handicapped ramp around the side. I wouldn't be caught dead with you scooting backwards on your butt."

There were only two people in the room when they found where they were supposed to be. One was a stocky, balding man in his early sixties, reading a magazine. The other was a rather perky-looking young man sitting behind the desk at the front. He got up when Jane and Shelley came in.

"I was hoping more of you would come," he said, flashing a handsome smile. "The article in the local paper about Ms. Jackson's accident must have made a lot of the sign-ups think the class was canceled. What did you do to your foot?"

"I tripped on a curb, " Jane said.

"Oh," the man replied. "I'm Stefan Eckert. I'm the director of the Arts and Crafts part of the community project."

"You're teaching the class?" Shelley asked.

"Oh, no! I'm not remotely qualified. But I've got a

substitute. A very interesting man who just happened to be in town this week. I'm just here to catch people and assure them the class will go on. And sit in on as much of it as I can."

Jane introduced herself and Shelley and asked, "Do you know anything about Ms. Jackson's condition?"

Stefan Eckert shrugged. "I'm not family and the hospital won't tell me a thing."

The older man sitting at the back of the room was reading a copy of *Modern Maturity*. He closed the magazine and looked up at the others. "Hello. Glad to see other people here. I've really been looking forward to this class."

There was a faintly clanging noise in the hall and a fourth student arrived. A slightly heavy woman who looked to be in her mid-fifties, draped in layers of clattering beads, carrying a number of bags, and wearing clothes she must have had since the early seventies. Her neck and head were swathed in tie-dyed scarves. Pierced earrings made of a variety of feathers flapped at her ears. Copper bracelets banged against beaded bracelets and something looking like an old-fashioned charm bracelet. She carried a huge purse slung over her shoulder, a pack tied around her waist, and a violently colored canvas bag.

"Hello, Hello! Oh!" she bellowed as she spotted Jane and rushed over. "You poor darling! What have you done to yourself? A cast and everything. Are you in pain? Here, let me help you sit down and get the weight off that foot."

"No, no. I'm fine. Really. It doesn't hurt very much at all," Jane said, alarmed by the attention.

But her protestations did her no good. The woman dropped her purse and canvas bag on a chair, both of which instantly spilled out paperback books, most of which seemed to have the word "conspiracy" in the title, pamphlets, paper napkins, three matchbooks, several flower seed packets, half a dozen colored pens, a sketchbook, more odd jewelry, prescription blanks, receipts, nail files, one very dirty gardening glove, a small wrench, a computer cord, a small box of Q-tips, and what looked like an adult-sized version of a child's sippy cup half-full of a purple liquid.

Ignoring the mess around her feet, she said, "Here, darling. Sit down. I'll get you a chair to put your foot up and you'll tell me how you did this to yourself. Ursula Appledorn at your service."

Jane was somewhat roughly thrust into a folding chair and Ursula grabbed her leg and plopped it on another chair, and pulled up yet another chair facing Jane and flung herself into it and leaned forward.

"So?" she said.

"I tripped over a curbing," Jane said, thoroughly cowed.

Ursula shook her head. "No, darling. There has to be more to the story. And if there isn't, there should be. These things happen for a reason, you know. Everything is part of a vast chain of events that weaves us all together. Nice casting job, but a bit tight around the toes," she said, looking at Jane's foot as she started

28

gathering up her belongings from the floor.

Jane cast a helpless look at Shelley, who just grinned and said, "I was with her and it was sheer clumsiness."

"But even so, there was a reason," Ursula insisted. "I was a nurse in 'Nam," she added, as if this explained everything. "And I can tell you there's a LOT the government is concealing. Why, the Denver airport alone—"

Fortunately, two more people came into the room, and Ursula turned her attention to them, though less enthusiastically than when she'd spotted Jane.

The first was a small, slim, precise woman with permed gray hair and a very upright carriage in a trim navy blue and white polka-dot dress. She glanced around at the small group, instinctively identified Stefan as the person in charge and said, "Is the class to take place?" in a tone that suggested that a simple, straightforward answer was required. "I'm Martha Winstead," she said to those assembled. "*Miss* Martha Winstead and I'm signed up."

Stefan knew his place and when he'd met his match. "Yes, Miss Winstead. We've met before," he said obediently.

Miss Winstead said, "Of course we have." She nodded curtly and sat down primly in the front, folding her small, somewhat knobby hands neatly over her handbag. Her exposed forearms were tan, but the hands were white. Apparently a gardener who always wore gloves.

The man who followed her in obviously wasn't with

her. He was tall, wore serious spectacles, and had a professorial stoop that went with his leather-elbow-patched jacket. "You're Eckert?"

"Yessir. You must be Dr. Eastman. We're all so glad you were able to interrupt your busy schedule to fill in for Ms. Jackson."

"While I was surprised you didn't contact me first," he said, "I've known Julie for years and couldn't refuse to fill in for her at this terrible time. I'm used to lecturing knowledgeable graduate students, however, not amateurs."

Jane bridled at the way he said "amateurs," as if it were a slightly obscene word. Someone gave a small and very ladylike snort. Jane guessed it was Miss Martha Winstead. It wasn't nearly raucous enough to be Ursula.

Ursula herself promptly spoke up, though she hadn't been addressed. "My good sir, most of the great discoveries of mankind were made by amateurs, though that fact is often covered up." She waved her arm victoriously and an eyeglass repair kit fell out of her sleeve. "Intelligent amateurs can often see on overview what experts are too deeply into precious details to see. 'Amateur' is a flattering term."

"This isn't getting off to a good start," Jane whispered to Shelley.

"Probably more interesting than a 'lecture,' though," Shelley replied just as quietly. "This looks like a man who could bore us to sleep in five minutes or less."

Another man entered the room and aborted any reply

30

the professor might have made by asking, "Is this the botany class?" He was around forty years old and looked as if his slacks and shirt, as well as his thinning hair, had just been starched and ironed a moment ago. He had a round, shining clean face, eyeglasses that gleamed, and highly polished shoes.

Stefan Eckert said, "It is. But our scheduled instructor has been injured and we have a wonderful substitute who has graciously volunteered to fill in. Time is getting away from us, folks. I suggest we start and if anyone else joins us, they can just slip in and catch up. I want to introduce our guest speaker and then each of you will give your name and a brief explanation of why you're interested in this course."

The well-groomed newcomer took a chair at the front of the room and found himself next to Martha Winstead. "Miss Winstead!" he exclaimed. "I never expected to find you here."

"Why is that, Mr. Jones?" she asked curtly. Jane noticed that the woman's hands tightened on the handle of her purse.

He looked confused for a moment as to how to reply, then said, "Well, your gardening is so . . . so haphazard . . . I just thought you wouldn't really be interested."

Miss Martha Winstead gave him a smile that could have frozen over a volcano and said, "Haphazard. How very interesting."

"If you wish to take notes, I have a few spiral notebooks here that the local nursery contributed," Stefan said in a shaky voice. "And some pens from my father's office supply store," he added with desperate good cheer.

Four

Stefan took a protective stance behind the desk at the front of the room and read off an introduction to the speaker. It was a long list, obviously prepared by the professor himself, of incomprehensible degrees and honors, initials of presumably high-status organizations Dr. Stewart Eastman belonged to or founded or served as president of, and awards Jane had never heard of. Stefan must have pronounced a number of them incorrectly, because every now and then Dr. Eastman, standing next to the desk, cringed ever so slightly.

When Stefan stepped aside with a little bow, Dr. Eastman took his place, saying, "Since Mr. Eckert suggested introductions, we might as well proceed with them. Tell us who you are and why you signed on for this class. You first," he said, pointing to Jane.

She gave her name and added, somewhat idiotically in her own view, "I've spent most of my adult life raising children and pets, but as a once-upon-a-time child of a member of the diplomatic corps, I lived my childhood all over the world and saw many gardens and have always thought I'd like very much to have one of my own. So far I've only taken the slightest stab at it and want to learn more."

Shelley was next. "My adult life has been much like Jane's, but my children are growing older and more independent, giving me time to develop other interests. Gardening is high on my list of priorities. I'm Jane's next-door neighbor."

Jane smiled to herself. This was a surprisingly meek self-description of Shelley. Shelley had finally been caught out in something she knew very little about and couldn't even fake the dominant role that normally suited and served her so very well. Shelley made a tiny shoulder movement like a shrug or shiver, as if she were reading Jane's mind.

Charles Jones, the terribly neat, clean, freshly pressed man, was next. He stood up like a good student and explained that he was a computer programmer and spent his leisure time in botanical pursuits and hoped they all lived close enough to form car pools and take a look at each other's gardens this week as a part of their studies.

There was a low mumble of agreement. Jane, however, was horrified. Her yard was very nearly a blank canvas. Every spring she swore she'd plant some gardens and fertilize the lawn. She never quite got around to it soon enough. She'd have to get Mike to clean up after Willard since she hadn't been outside with the pooper-scooper lately, and she'd have to bring in a bunch of potted annuals to look as if she had actually made an attempt at gardening this year. Mike could help her plant a few things since his summer job was at a plant nursery.

". . . and," Charles added, "I happen to be a next-door neighbor of Miss Winstead. I think you'd find our gardens an interesting contrast." He sounded smug and sat down neatly, tucking his trousers up at the knees to keep the knife edge.

Miss Winstead spoke in turn. She didn't stand. "I spent a great deal of my life as a professional librarian, and by a fortunate and unexpected circumstance of an inheritance from my great-aunt, was able to continue my librarian work as a volunteer and spend more time on my lifelong interest in gardening. Mr. Jones is quite correct in saying that our gardens are a contrast. I hope we adopt his suggestion." She smiled icily again at Jones.

The older man who'd been reading a magazine when Jane and Shelley arrived finally got up and spoke. "My name is Arnold Waring. My friends call me Arnie and I wish the rest of you would." He cleared his throat. "My late wife, Darlene, was a real gardener and she fixed up our house and yard just perfect. You should have seen her out in the backyard, pulling up weeds and tending her precious posies with a smile and a song."

Jane knew she was meant to feel touched, but had the urge to laugh. There was something so Victorian—or maybe vaudevillian—about that speech. It sounded for all the world like something from a Monty Python sketch.

"She's been gone a while now," Arnie went on. "And I've tried to keep everything just like she had it as a tribute to her memory. But I'm not very good at it, so I thought . . . ?" His voice trailed off and he sat down quickly, folding his beefy arms as if to protect himself.

"What a dear story, Arnie. And how good it was of you to share it with us," Ursula said. She stood up and said, "I'm here because I'm part of the cosmos. We're all living, breathing, nurture-seeking beings, and gardens must be part of our nature. They are nature in their finest refinement."

Two paper clips fell from her and tinkled to the floor. "And I'm interested, as I'm sure we all are," she added, looking around at everyone for possible early signs of disagreement, "in what part the government has in this area. They have their greedy fingers in every other aspect of our lives."

She smiled and sat down on a fork that had fallen out of one of her bags. "Oops," she giggled, stuffing it back into her enormous purse.

Dr. Eastman looked around the room for anyone he'd missed, and Stefan said, "I'm a student, too, sir. I would have been here even if Julie hadn't—" He started over. "I want to put in a little pool in my yard and I'm confused about plants and fish and snails and how much you have to have of each and what will live over the winter." He smiled. "I'm from the South and haven't gotten used to Chicago winters yet. Don't know that I ever will."

There was a tap on the door and Stefan, now having drifted to the back of the room to take a seat, turned to open it. Somebody gasped. The woman who entered looked a great deal like Julie Jackson.

She glanced around, unsure of herself. "I'm Geneva Jackson. Julie Jackson's sister. I'm sorry to interrupt, but thought you might like a report on how she's doing since you might have read about her being attacked."

To a polite chorus of yeses, she replied, "She's still in intensive care and is almost conscious part of the time. Enough to move her hands and make sounds. The doctors, including my husband, who is a neurologist, say she's making terrific progress and could make a quite good recovery, given time and luck. Or not, to be frank."

"And you've kept your own name," Ursula piped up. "I like that in a modern woman. Of course, all women's maiden names are really a man's. Their father's. In other cultures, matrilineal ones, it's different. Everyone takes the mother's name, which is far more appropriate and scientifically significant because everyone's DNA patterns follow through in the maternal line."

Shelley felt it was time to take control since no one else was except Ursula. She got up, threaded her way through the chairs, and took Geneva's arm. "Why don't you sit in for a bit to cool off and rest? Dr. Eastman is about to begin his lecture and you might be interested. You look like you need a break from the hospital."

Geneva gratefully sat down and said to the group somewhat apologetically, "I'm a disaster at hospitals. I try to jolly people along and only drive them mad. My husband is staying by her bedside and is far more qualified, and asked me to leave, actually," she said with a self-deprecating smile to the group. "Will it be all right with you, Dr. Eastman, if I sit in?"

"Perfectly all right," he answered pleasantly. "And I'm glad to hear your sister is improving. We've just told each other about ourselves and our interest in this class. I think the others would like to know about you."

He was speaking to her as if they were already acquainted, Jane thought. Perhaps they were.

"My sister is part of a team that investigates claims for plant patents. I'm in another part of the business. Julie does freelance lab work and cuttings of plants under consideration for patents whenever there appears to be a difficulty with the patent. I have a farm in the high plains of Colorado and am one of the testers throughout this country, Canada, and Mexico for her. I'm sure Dr. Eastman will explain all of this to you."

Geneva Jackson sat back a bit more comfortably, signifying that she was ready to listen.

Five

Dr. Eastman drew himself up and said, "It's difficult to know exactly where to begin. Many gardeners have heard of plant patents, and mistakenly believe this is a recent development along with cloning. That's not true. The United States Plant Patent Act was enacted in the late 1920s—"

"Nineteen-thirty," Miss Martha Winstead said in her soft but clear librarian's voice. "In late May."

He glared at her, didn't argue with her or accept her correction, and went on, reading from a card, "It states that whoever invents or discovers and asexually reproduces any distinct and new variety of plant, including cultivated sports, mutants, hybrids, and newly found seedlings, other than a tuber-propagated plant or plant found in an uncultivated state, may obtain a patent therefore."

They all stared at him blankly.

"Would you repeat that slowly so we can write it down?" Ursula asked, fumbling on the floor where her notepad and pens were and stuffing other random bits that had fallen out again back into her purse.

Dr. Eastman did so. "I can tell that some of these terms are unfamiliar to some of you. 'Asexual reproduction' is probably one. This means creating a new plant from an old one in almost any manner, *except* by planting seeds. You could root a cutting of the plant, use a section of the root or tuber to grow a new one, divide a bulb, air-layer a branch of a shrub or tree, or take a bulblet from a corm. The reason is that the new plant that grew in any of these ways would be the exact genetic duplicate of the original plant."

Seeing some comprehending nods, he went on. "A seed, on the other hand, represents sexual reproduction—a mix of chromosomes from two plants. And this, in fact, is a good place to start the process. If you want, for example, a special color of impatiens, you could make many pollen crosses, wait for the seeds to develop, and see if any of them produced the color you wanted. If one did, you could take many cuttings because impatiens roots easily from cuttings. Or if you wanted to develop a bigger or bushier impatiens, you'd cross-pollinate the biggest ones you can find that were also the color you're seeking."

"But you said the Plant Patent Act doesn't apply to seeds," Shelley said.

"And I also said that impatiens are easy to root from cuttings," Dr. Eastman said. "If you got a spirea-sized bush of impatiens, it might have the same rooting capacity of the shrub. Or it might not. That's the point of hybridizing. Some methods fail, precious few are roaring successes."

He glanced around, fairly satisfied that most of his audience appeared to be catching on. "Naturally, you have to keep detailed records of each cross, the result, and a full description of each plant involved. This mass of data must be submitted with the plant patent application. If you just sent in a description of a plant and a cutting or picture or little potted example, without significant records, you'd certainly be rejected and told to do it right."

"Doesn't this take a terrifically long time?" Jane asked.

"It often does," Eastman said. "The initial work is tedious and you have to wait for a seed to grow, mature, and go to seed before you know what you've got. But professional breeders have many projects going on at the same time, so it's not as if you sit around reading the newspaper for a year or two, waiting for the seedling to grow to maturity.

"The next stage is to find growers that are called triallers, because they do the trials. Breeders have . . . well, let us say, somewhat secret and well-trusted relationships with many triallers. I work in the north of Illinois. I have very private contracts with plantsmen who have isolated areas for growing in the high plains, the deep South, the northwest rain forest area, West Texas, Maine, the Appalachians, and desert environments. I send cuttings or bulblets or whatever parts of the plant I'm testing that qualify as asexual reproduction to the environments I think will be suitable. And oftentimes to areas I *don't* think are suitable as well, simply because a breeder can be surprised by an unexpected trait of the plant that he wasn't cross-breeding for."

Someone must have looked confused by this. Eastman looked at somebody behind Jane and said, "Suppose your hybridized impatiens turned out to be surprisingly hardy. Southern testers wouldn't know this, but someone north of here might realize that this particular impatiens could take at least a light frost without falling over because the cell structure collapses at thirty-two degrees."

He went on to other examples, and after another half hour when he sensed that the audience was getting information overload, he said, "That's all my lecturing for today. I have a little booklet I put together explaining what I've talked about this session that I'll hand out for you to read over and absorb. We'll do questions about the material and go on to the next stage at tomorrow's lesson."

"What about the garden tours?" Miss Martha Winstead asked.

"That's what we'll plan out during the rest of this session. And then we'll have a little 'show and tell' as well. I'd like to leave Mrs. Jeffry and Mrs. Nowack for last since they seem to be in the earliest stages of gardening and will be able to benefit from seeing the other gardens first. And we'll do Miss Winstead and Mr. Jones on the same day as they also live next door to each other. I have a house here in the neighborhood I use when I'm visiting my children and grandchildren and giving lectures in Chicago. But I'm not as familiar with this area as the rest of you, so I leave it up to the group to plan the schedule."

Everybody exchanged addresses and it turned out that nobody lived terribly far away. It would be simple to do two gardens a day in the second half of class. Simple in theory, of course, until other factors came into it. Miss Winstead wanted to go first because she had something blooming that wouldn't last beyond Tuesday or Wednesday. Ursula Appledorn lived near a house that had a huge garage sale nearly every Thursday, and parking at her home that day would be impossible.

Dr. Eastman waited with barely controlled impatience while a great deal of time was wasted discussing routes, and days, and car-pool participants, the students occasionally wandering far off the subject entirely to speculate about weather, road conditions, and garden-tool storage as well as to make some random comments on hairdressers, some controversial decisions the city council was considering, and What Our Youth Are Coming To.

Shelley, in an agony over the others' lack of control and organizational abilities, took over. "Here, I've listened to everyone and drawn up a schedule. Pass it around and copy it down."

She rather violently ripped a page out of her spiral notebook and thrust it at Ursula, who had caused the most meanderings.

"Are we all sorted out now?" Dr. Eastman asked.

Everybody looked at Shelley.

"We had better be," she said firmly.

Miss Martha Winstead, a woman of the same cut, nodded to Shelley approvingly.

"Very well, I'll just let my assistant know we're ready for the next item," Eastman said, going to the door and calling down the hall to someone named Bryan.

Bryan turned out to be a large, faintly stupid-looking teenager with very serious muscles and extraordinary balance. He carried a large box as lightly and carefully as Jane would have handled an egg carton. He set it down on the desk. It was a box with a cover that went almost to the bottom of the lower box. Sort of like a giant candy box. Bryan and Dr. Eastman each eased up one side of it.

42

On the platform of the lower box was a miniature garden. Something spiky in the middle and a frothy mass of what Jane thought was artemisia around the edge. But what was between these was confusing.

Small compact plants with jagged dark green foliage and coral pink flowers.

"What are the pink ones?" Shelley asked.

Dr. Eastman leaned forward and said in a thrilling voice, "Marigolds."

"Marigolds aren't pink. They're all colors of gold, cream, and orange," Ursula said, getting up to take a good look. The rest of the group followed her example.

"These *are* marigolds," Dr. Eastman said firmly. "I'm sorry I can't share them with you because I've applied for the patent, but they're not available to the public yet."

Jane wasn't all that knowledgeable about plants, but she knew marigolds well. They were one of the few annuals that could survive her neglect and were cheap enough to buy a lot of. "Could we touch them?" she asked.

"Certainly," Eastman replied.

Jane pinched a leaf and smelled her fingers. It was the distinct odor of marigolds. The foliage was exactly right—dark, glossy green with jagged edges. It was the color that was astonishing. The flowers were certainly shaped exactly like marigolds, but looked as if they must have been dyed and stuck on with wires. She touched a flower and it was lush and alive. Could they have been injected along the stem or soil with that color?

She remembered the Queen Anne's lace along the hedgerows of her grandmother's farm. She and her sister Marty would pick them and Grandmother would let them put the stems in colored water and sometimes little bottles of ink, and the creamy white flowers changed to that color.

Could you do that to a cream-colored marigold?

Or was it truly a coral pink marigold? Surely Dr. Eastman, who was so knowledgeable about plant patents, wouldn't play the sort of trick Jane was thinking of. Turning around, she glanced at Geneva Jackson, who had remained in her chair at the back of the room. Geneva was smiling.

"How did you do that?" Miss Martha Winstead asked in awed tones.

"Through long and tedious cross-breeding," Dr. Eastman said. "Tomorrow I'll bring a copy of my data that you can glance over to get an idea of how it is arranged and the detailing that's necessary as well as what the patent applications look like."

"This is truly sensational, and that's not a word I use lightly," Martha said. "When will they be available to the public?"

"Not for another two years or maybe three. Since they have to be asexually produced, I'll have to hire out the growing to all the plant growers I can find. Fortunately, we have the advantage of cloning now. It's far more expensive, but much faster. Marigolds aren't prone to rooting from slips."

Nobody in the room could tear their eyes away from the astonishing plants.

"I'll be the first to buy them," Ursula said. "They're amazing and will look so good in with my herbs."

Eastman nodded to Bryan, the helper, who carefully set the top of the box back in place and carried it away.

Six

As Shelley and Jane headed out from the community center to have lunch at their favorite Mexican restaurant, they gushed about the extraordinary pink marigold.

"Just think how much work went into creating such a thing," Shelley said. "I would never have the patience to do all that. Didn't someone have a long-running contest for a pure white marigold?"

"I remember that, too. I don't think they ever got anything whiter than a light cream color."

"Nor would I even have thought of trying to get a pink one if I were in that business."

"You know, that's the thing about this morning that surprised me most," Jane said. "That it *is* a business. A very serious one. I always thought that new plants were much easier to come up with than it appears. There must be big money involved or nobody'd wait years."

"I wouldn't be surprised. When the pink marigold

hits the nurseries, it'll sell in millions. I wonder how we could ask about the money part."

Jane looked down her cast, which was already getting grubby around the toes. "Did you notice that Geneva Jackson didn't come up to look at the plants?"

"I didn't. But she has more important things on her mind."

"But she was smiling as we gawked."

"Was she really?" Shelley said, taking a corner so fast that it made the wheels of her van squeal.

"Didn't you have the feeling that Dr. Eastman knew her pretty well?" Jane asked in a shaky voice. The worst thing about the broken foot was having to be Shelley's passenger.

"Which one of them?"

"Both Julie and Geneva, it sounded like."

"Come to think of it, it did seem that way," Shelley said, beating out another van for the last parking place in front of the restaurant and waving cheerily at the other driver.

"You can't park here," Jane said. "It's a handicapped parking spot and I forgot to bring along the sticker they gave me to hang on the rearview mirror."

"You're obviously handicapped, if only for a little while."

"I think Geneva might be one of his 'secret' growers. If so, it would explain why she didn't come look at the plants. She's probably seen hundreds of them."

Jane struggled out of the van, coming down a little

too hard on her injured foot. But it was worth it to be free of Shelley's driving.

They got their favorite booth near the front window and made much of studying the menu, even though both of them had it pretty well memorized from their many previous visits.

The waitress saw Jane's crutches and exclaimed, "What in the world did you do to yourself?"

"I tripped on a curb."

The waitress looked blank for a minute and finally said, "Oh."

Jane got the taco salad with the chili mixed in, and Shelley let herself go with a chicken chimichanga. When the waitress had gone, Shelley asked, "Do you think the attack on Julie Jackson had anything to do with her job?"

"I've been wondering the same thing," Jane said. "I'm not clear on exactly how she fits into this business, though. Geneva said they had a professional relationship as well as being sisters. Is Julie, like Dr. Eastman, a plant breeder?"

Shelley shrugged. "Eastman suggested that she was some sort of patent cop. Checking out suspicious claims. Only he said 'questionable,' I think. She didn't appear to have anything especially interesting growing in her yard."

"But we didn't see the backyard."

"True. Do you think Mel knows exactly what it is that she does?"

"You heard all he said," Jane replied. "She had a sort

of laboratory/office in her basement with lots of filing cabinets and some plants under lights. I think that's what he said. I was too obsessed with my foot to pay much attention."

"We need to find out exactly where Julie comes into the process. I might have misunderstood what Dr. Eastman was saying about her job. Maybe this attack on her comes back to money, like we were discussing before."

"In what way?" Jane asked.

"I don't know, because we have no idea what sort of money is involved. Or who gets it and how. I really want to know about that part of it. So many crimes come down to money."

"Then why didn't her attacker take anything?" Jane asked.

"We don't know he or she didn't," Shelley said. "And Geneva would be about the only one who could guess what might be missing. And even she might not be able to determine that."

"Mom, why did you get such a boring cast?" Jane's daughter said with just a hint of a French accent as she came into the Jeffry living room later that afternoon.

"I wasn't offered anything else," Jane said. "Would you get me a glass of iced tea, Katie? It's in the fridge."

"I've got something better." There were a couple of faint z's in "something."

Katie rummaged in her jeans pocket and pulled out a folded sheet of paper.

"What is this?" Jane said. "Oh, pretty flower stickers. They actually look like color photos. I could stick them around the screen of my computer."

Katie threw herself into an armchair and said, "Oh, Mom," in a highly critical tone.

"Wouldn't they?"

"Mom, they're for your cast. Nobody has a boring cast. You have to have your friends sign it, and if you know an artist, you ask him to draw or paint a picture on it. And even if you don't, you put stickers on it." She'd temporarily lost her fake accent. "One guy at school with a broken arm had a really cool one. His mother wove ribbons like a plaid design on his and stuck them down somehow. So when do you get it off?"

"Before it gets really filthy, I hope. The doctor didn't say. Just that I had to come back in two weeks to have it X-rayed again."

"Cool. They'll have to cut it with a saw to do that," Katie said. "Can I come along?"

"My leg or the cast? A real *saw?*"

"I do not know, *ma mère*. I'll ask my friend."

Katie had spent the first two weeks of summer vacation in France with her best friend, Jenny, and Jenny's parents, who had begged to have Katie along so Jenny wouldn't be bored with the sight-seeing they planned to do. Jane had been more than glad to spring for the plane fare to get Katie out of her hair for part of the summer. Katie'd made no effort to get a summer job, not even at her usual summer haunt, the town swimming pool. Something about the chlorine ruining her hair. Even before the trip idea came up, Jane had dreaded having her underfoot and at loose ends for the whole three months.

The trip hadn't quite turned out as Jane imagined. Katie had fallen in love with all things French. The French were "civilized" and ate dinner at ten at night. She'd been saving up the dinners Jane made to warm back up and eat just before she went to bed. She wanted her mother to study wine sauces and get some good veal. Quite a change from her earlier views of meat, and veal in particular.

"Katie, you're going to have to take over some of the cooking for us," Jane said. "It's too hard for me to get around the kitchen right now. But no veal. Why don't we make up some menus? It's time you learned how to cook."

"What about Mike? He's older than I am. Make him learn to cook."

"He doesn't care what he eats."

The kitchen door had opened and closed while they were discussing this. "Are you talking about me?" Mike said, coming in the living room with a girl in tow. "Mom, this is Kipsy Topper. We met today at the garden place where I'm working for the summer."

Jane had to make a serious effort to keep her jaw from dropping. Kipsy Topper, if that was really her name, which Jane was certain it wasn't, was the last thing she'd ever expected Mike to bring home. She had flame-colored hair. Or maybe it was a wig. Sort of like a big Raggedy Ann doll. Her eyebrows and nose were pierced and she was wearing what looked like a very flimsy slip over baggy jeans. There was a snake tattoo on her skinny shoulder. She could have been fourteen or twenty-four. Either way, too young or too old for Mike. And much too bizarre. He'd always gone for the blond cheerleader types.

"Kipsy . . ." Jane said, gulped, and went on, "how nice to meet you."

She was looking at Mike as she spoke. He was smiling blandly.

"If you're talking about food," he said, "Kipsy and I are going to a Thai restaurant this evening where she works part-time. She was buying plants for the owner to decorate the place. They're in my truck. We're taking them over now. Be back late probably."

Jane sat thunderstruck as Mike whisked Kipsy out of the house.

"Wow!" Katie said.

"Is that a good wow or a bad one?" Jane asked.

"Mom," Katie said critically, "you can't go on judging people by how they look. That's so frumpy and it's bigoted besides."

"I certainly *can* judge people when they make an effort to look like freaks," Jane said. "That says something about their personality."

Katie couldn't answer this, so she just sniffed with contempt and said, "I thought she looked cool. I might do that to my hair."

"Over my dead body," Jane said. "Or yours. I'll let

you drive us to the grocery store on your learner's permit if you promise not to scare me."

"I think Mike has gone over the edge," Jane said to Shelley later. "You should have *seen* this girl."

"I did," Shelley said. "Through my kitchen window as they came in your house. I wanted to go find my Denise and lock her in a closet until she's twenty-five. Maybe thirty. Where did Mike find her?"

"At the nursery where he's working. She was buying plants for the restaurant where she works. The owner must have taste as bad as hers to turn her loose to make decorating decisions, considering how she's decorated herself."

"Don't worry. Mike's a bright kid. He won't fall for her," Shelley said.

"What if you're wrong?" Jane whined. "Can you imagine having a daughter-in-law like that? Think of the wedding. Probably held in a Thai restaurant with bridesmaids in underwear or saris. Or under some bridge downtown next door to a body-piercing empo-rium."

"Maybe he just dragged her in to show you a novelty," Shelley said.

"Dear God, I hope so."

"Jane, you're the one going over the edge. He appar-ently just met her. Don't go worrying about a wedding. You'll see that he doesn't marry until he finishes col-lege."

Seven

Jane puttered around in the kitchen awkwardly, trying to think what would be easiest to cook for dinner. A roast maybe. Just put it in a bag and drag it out later. But that would take two hands. Could she balance herself well enough without at least one crutch to do that? Hamburgers on the grill? Nope, too many steps down to the patio.

As she cruised the fridge, there was a banging on her kitchen door and Ursula Appledorn walked in. Jane wished she weren't so careless about locking up and that non–family members or close friends would not assume an unlocked door meant you didn't have to knock. But she put on a welcoming smile because that was how she'd been raised.

"You need good food and I've brought it to you. Hold the screen door for me," Ursula said, going back to an even more disreputable station wagon than Jane's.

In a moment she was back with a large paper carton that she started unloading on Jane's kitchen counter.

"Hominy," she said of a covered dish she slapped down. "Lots of nutrients. Some dandelion greens from my own yard, barely cooked so the vitamins are still in them. Be sure to drink the juice. Tons of calcium and potassium. Good for broken bones."

"Uh . . . Ursula, I'm planning to have hamburgers for dinner."

"Meat?" Ursula was stunned. "I didn't think anyone actually ate meat these days. The government demands that so many cancer-causing chemicals are in it."

"I think you might have that backwards. The government tries to make the farmers take out the chemicals," Jane said, examining the dandelion greens, which seemed to have a good many foreign objects that looked like insects cooked up with the greens. She hoped they were just flowers that had wilted to that stage.

"No, dear. The government is responsible for poisoning us. At the very least, you have to admit they allow it. Look at the strawberries that they let into this country. Death on a stem. And here's some totally natural bread. I made it myself out of organically grown potato flour and free-range eggs." The bread made a thunk like a brick being dropped.

"Ursula, I'm really not entirely helpless. I appreciate your thoughtfulness, but—"

"Think nothing of it, Jane. We're all in this together. I'm a nurse, you know. Well, I was a nurse until the government took away my license on a foolish pretense."

"What was the pretense?" Jane couldn't help but ask.

"Drug dealing," Ursula said calmly, taking the lid off a bowl of soybean curd with a greenish blue gravy over it that looked suspiciously like algae. "Ridiculous, of course. I didn't use any of the so-called controlled substances. Only natural herbs, spices, and minerals for my private patients. And they all thrived. Why, one got to be a hundred and one years old and left me all her money out of gratitude for making her last two years so stimulating. Now, sit down at the table and let me dish this all up for you."

By now Jane needed to sit down, but not to eat. Was this, she hoped, a onetime visit or did Ursula plan on forcing revolting food on her until her foot healed? Horrors!

Ursula rummaged in a drawer and brought up a battered kitchen spoon to ladle her creations onto a plate sitting on the counter. "There now, just taste. You'll feel ever so much better."

There was another knock on the door and Ursula ran to let Shelley in.

"Oh, Ms. Appledorn. I didn't know you were here." When Ursula turned away from her, Shelley winked at Jane.

Jane gave Shelley a *HELP ME!* look.

"I'm just giving Jane her dinner," Ursula said.

"What is that stuff?" Shelley asked, not disguising her distaste at the sight.

Ursula, more in pity than anger, explained all the items. Shelley listened and nodded and tried to hide a smile. "I'm not sure it's a good time for Jane to completely change her diet. She's under considerable stress, you know."

Ursula nodded. "That's why I brought the caraway-flavored hummus. Excellent for stress."

"Dear God," Jane whispered to herself.

"Actually, I was just coming to fetch Jane to come to

my house for dinner. I thought we'd have carryout Chinese."

"All that MSG!" Ursula said with terror. "That stuff can kill you."

"It hasn't yet," Shelley said calmly. "Jane and I thrive on it."

"I'm not really hungry," Jane said. "Why don't you put this in the fridge for later? A midnight snack, perhaps?"

By midnight she could probably hobble out to dump the stuff in the trash and pretend she'd polished it all off.

"Excellent idea. Just don't eat that Chinese stuff. Let's just sit down and get to know each other."

Shelley, standing behind Ursula, rolled her eyes. Jane sighed.

Ursula insisted on settling Jane on the couch in the living room and putting an afghan around her. "Ursula, it's summer," Shelley mentioned.

"But extra heat is good for almost every ailment. Take my word on this."

Shelley took a chair and so did Ursula. Then the three of them sat and stared at each other.

Ursula was the first to break the silence. "You do know about the Denver airport, don't you? The new one?"

"What's to know?" Jane asked. "Except that's a big place."

Ursula laughed bitterly. "Have you *seen* the murals?"

"The bright-colored ones near the baggage pickup? Yes, I saw them a couple years ago," Jane said.

"And they didn't disturb you?" Ursula asked.

Jane shrugged. "I wouldn't want them in my living room, but I wasn't disturbed by them."

"You should have studied them. They're all about Satanism." Ursula leaned forward and a paper clip fell off her from somewhere.

Shelley lifted an eyebrow skeptically.

"Yes, it's a conspiracy that was started by the Dauphin when he escaped to America and set up the Virginia Company, which meant all the money made in America would eventually go to England."

Jane cleared her throat. "Uh . . . wasn't the Dauphin French?" She almost added, *And wasn't the Virginia Company set up several centuries earlier?* But she was curious about where this was leading.

"By birth, of course, but he'd been rescued by Englishmen and owed his allegiance to them. So this trust has operated with the consent and encouragement of the Windsor family ever since then. The Queen of England actually owns most of Colorado, you know. Under a false name, of course. And she owns the land the Denver airport is on."

Shelley mumbled through the hand she was holding to her mouth to keep from laughing, "What's the false name?"

"Nobody knows," Ursula said. "Probably there are many false names for her."

Jane was having trouble keeping a straight face as

well. "Does the IRS know about this?"

"Naturally. They're part of the conspiracy. As is the CIA. And the Masons. They've been involved ever since the Templars were killed in France in the fifteenth century. But a few escaped and went to Ireland and started the Masonic order. The King of France wanted to kill them to get their fortune, and the fortune disappeared as well."

"I think you mean the fourteenth century," Jane said. "Thirteen oh nine or so?"

"Fourteenth or fifteenth, whatever. The capstone at the airport is a Masonic symbol, just like that one that is on our money. I don't know why people can't see the connection. All our so-called Founding Fathers were Masons. On the original architectural drawings of the airport, it said it was a 'control center for New World control.'"

"An awkward sentence to be sure. You've seen the plans?" Jane said. This was spinning out of control and no longer funny.

"Not personally," Ursula said, picking up a barrette that had worked its way out of her hair, "but I know people who know other people who have seen them. And then when you put this together with Cecil Rhodes—"

Shelley made a choking noise and hurried into the kitchen.

"Cecil Rhodes?" Jane repeated dimly.

"Yes, that was the whole idea of the Rhodes scholarships. To train Americans to think like Brits."

"I never knew," Jane said. "Ursula, it's awfully nice of you to have visited, but you'll have to excuse me. I have some letters to write and a couple birthday cards that have to go in the mail this evening."

"I'll run you to the post office—and speaking of the post office, they're part of it, too. Do you have any idea how many postal workers are Masons?"

Shelley was back, still pretending she had a little coughing fit. "I don't think Jane should really go anywhere right now. She needs to rest. I'll take her mail for her."

Ursula took this with good grace. Gathering up the huge purse and only dropping two cigarette lighters and a receipt, she said, "Get a good night's sleep and I'll see you two in the morning at class." She barged out, forgetting to even close the kitchen door.

Jane and Shelley sat back, not speaking, only sighing in unison.

A few seconds later, the screen door opened again and Ursula was back with three of the scrappiest paperback books Jane had ever seen. One was held together along the spine with strapping tape. All were stained and creased with crumbling covers.

"Here, ladies, read up. You'll find them fascinating." She dumped them on the coffee table and went off again, tossing a remark over her shoulder about needing to get them back someday.

This time Shelley followed her and, when Ursula's battered vehicle was out of sight, closed and locked the door.

"I've heard of people like her," Shelley said, sitting back down by Jane, "but never really believed the descriptions of them. Now we know that there are true nutcases roaming our very own neighborhood."

"She's really sort of frightening, isn't she?" Jane said seriously. "I mean, isn't she exactly the kind of nut who decides that a bunch of Boy Scouts are Nazi spies and poisons their milk to save the world?"

"I'm not sure. But she frightens me just the same. And if I weren't a bit scared of her, I'd still dislike her. She's one of those people who get everything wrong, and when corrected, merely ignore the correction. Not that I go around correcting people if I can help it," she added with a smile.

"Funny. I hadn't noticed that about you." Jane smiled back.

"You've absolutely got to keep all your doors locked and stay in the back of the house where nobody can see you tottering around," Shelley warned. "She's latched on to you and *will* be back."

"Maybe I can make it clear that I don't want help?"

"You can't. People like that are incapable of being insulted or brushed off. She's probably gone through dozens, if not hundreds, of potential friends with her loony pronouncements. People have probably moved from their homes in the middle of the night to escape her and gone to live in Venezuela under assumed names."

"Oh, Shelley," Jane whined. "My life's falling apart before my eyes. My foot is broken; my son is out to

60

dinner with a freak of a girl; and I have a nutcase groupie."

Shelley just shook her head. "Such is life," she said.

Eight

Jane was getting ready for bed when the phone rang. It was Ursula again. "Jane, have you eaten your dinner yet?"

Gritting her teeth with irritation for a moment, Jane said in a cool formal voice, "Not yet."

"You must eat, dear. You need all the nutrients you can get."

Jane drew a deep breath and tried to overcome her upbringing in the diplomatic corps.

"Ursula, I know you mean well, but I'm an intelligent adult and can take perfectly good care of myself."

As Shelley had predicted, Ursula took no offense. "I know you are. I'm just concerned about you."

"Thank you, but I'm already in bed and almost asleep, so I have to hang up now."

Jane put the phone down before Ursula could reply.

She knew she'd been rude, but knew of no other way to get rid of this extremely annoying person. Especially when she had other disturbing things on her mind.

The doctor had told her she must be very careful of her foot. The fracture was clear across the large outside bone but still in place. If it shifted, he warned, they'd have to operate and pin it back in place and she'd be on crutches for a very long time.

And her older son was going out with a girl who had deliberately made herself look like a freak. She always thought he had abnormally good sense. Had she merely fooled herself?

Her daughter was acting like she knew everything there was to know about France after a two-week visit, which was annoying because Jane had spent several years total living in France herself when she was a girl and her diplomatic corps parents had been stationed there. Jane's own dislike of a gypsy life with no real home had convinced her that her children would have normal lives and stay in the same home until they were grown. Maybe she'd made a mistake in that.

And besides everything else that was bothering her, her foot hurt. Her arms hurt from fighting the crutches, even the other leg hurt because she was having to put all her weight on it, and her back was having alarming little twinges. When she was a teenager, she could have coped with this, but forty-year-old bodies reacted badly to change.

Then her mind turned to the reactions of others. That was a revelation to her. Perfect strangers had asked her how she did that to herself, and all sounded disappointed when she admitted she simply fell off a curbing.

She finally was able to smile to herself. Maybe she could spice up the story a bit. She crawled into bed, trying very hard not to kick the cats, who were eyeing her suspiciously, and fell asleep thinking of other explanations for the cast.

She woke suddenly an hour later when she heard the front door open and close and Mike's distinctive foot-steps coming upstairs. She flipped on her bedside light and called softly to him.

"Don't forget to set your alarm," she said when he poked his head around her bedroom door. "You're really late coming in."

"I always set my alarm, Mom," he said with a grin.

He knew her too well. "Okay, okay. Did you have a nice evening?"

"Fair to middling. Kipsy's an interesting girl. Night, Mom."

Interesting? Jane brooded. She didn't get back to sleep for another half hour.

"Mike says Kipsy is 'interesting,'" Jane said to Shelley on the phone in the morning.

"Interesting is a long way from fascinating," Shelley replied. "How's your foot feeling this morning?"

"About the same. I'm more comfortable in bed than anywhere else, though. And I can't let myself turn into a sloth. We are going to class, aren't we?"

"If you're sure you're up to it. Will you be able to walk around gardens without mowing them down with your crutches or going facedown in the begonias?"

"I hope so. I better get moving."

Jane used the waterproof tape Shelley had bought for her to fasten the plastic bag around her leg to shower.

No water came in the top, but when she finished, she realized the waterproof tape had stuck violently to the back of her knee and hurt like the devil to yank off. What's more, the bag had sprung a leak at the bottom, and the part of the cast near her toes was wet today. She'd have to buy a whole box of plastic bags at this rate.

She'd been wearing her two best casual skirts most of the time since breaking her foot. Today she'd have to shift to slacks or jeans. But she discovered that the cast made her leg too fat for slacks and had to wear the baggy shorts with the pockets on the thighs after all. Still, she managed to get ready on time, by merely whisking a brush through her hair haphazardly and slapping on basic makeup with rough abandon.

"What happened to your hair?" Shelley asked when Jane had bottom-bumped her way down the kitchen porch steps and climbed awkwardly into Shelley's van.

"Not nearly enough," Jane replied. "Whose gardens are we seeing today? I've forgotten my list."

"The instructor's second home over on Linden Street. And then Ursula's yard."

Jane shuddered at the name. "She called me late last night to see if I had eaten her stuff. I was honest enough to tell her no. And brave enough to stand up for myself. I told her I appreciated her concern, but could take care of myself."

"Not exactly standing up for yourself very strongly. 'Please, PLEASE, leave me alone' might have done it better."

64

"Frankly, I'm afraid of finding out how high her insult threshold is. Should I exceed it, she could be a more formidable enemy than would-be friend."

"You aren't going to let yourself get sucked into a friendship with her, are you?"

"No. Of course not. I've put up with some pretty obnoxious people that you wouldn't have put up with, but I'm not a complete moron."

As they pulled up in front of the community center, a strange man, seeing Jane struggle to get out the door of the van, rushed to help her.

"How did you do that to yourself?" he asked.

"An elephant pushed me off a circus van," Jane said. "Thank you so much for helping me."

The man looked astonished and said, "Wow!"

"A circus van?" Shelley hissed as they went up the ramp.

"I've got a list of interesting answers. I knew he'd like that one better than anybody's liked the truth."

The class was assembled when they entered the room. All but Ursula. Dr. Eastman, with his prize pink marigolds on display again, had just begun to speak and waited while Jane thrashed the crutches among the chairs and seated herself. Maybe she had insulted Ursula and she wasn't coming to the class any longer, Jane thought.

But her hopes were dashed a minute later. Ursula bustled in, speaking before she was completely in the room because a backpack strap had caught in the door. "I'm sorry to be late, but I was doing last-minute tidying of my garden." She smiled around the room, waiting for admiration.

"Let's begin now," Dr. Eastman said.

Today his talk was about the patent process, using words like "taxon" and "genotype" and "tissue culture" and "approach grafting." Jane was at sea and didn't want to be the dummy who asked what taxon meant. Besides, the outside of her calf was itching like crazy. She pulled a pencil out of her pocket and ran the pencil down inside the cast to try to reach the itch.

Suddenly Ursula, who'd sat behind her, reached forward and snatched the pencil from her hand. "Lead poisoning," she whispered just loudly enough for everyone to hear her. "Wait a minute."

She rummaged in one of her bags and brought up a very long, fat crochet hook with a nicely rounded tip. "Use this."

Jane tried to pretend to be listening avidly, while scrabbling around inside the cast, chasing the itch.

Finally the instructor came back to plain English, saying, "The plant must remain stable in its qualities through a great many means of asexual reproduction, such as cuttings, grafting, and budding."

He went on, "If you're interested in trying to get a patent, there are a number of pieces of valuable advice. One: get early and expert confidential advice from someone who really knows plant patent law, and be prepared to pay for it."

"He's trying to convince us to try this so he can make money off us," Shelley whispered.

"Fat chance," Jane whispered back.

"Two: Remember that country boundaries are imaginary for plants. You should look into worldwide patents and make yourself familiar with foreign catalogs. Three: Keep your work as secret as possible. Do your climatic testing with trusted professionals. Don't give out samples to friends. And four: If someone learns of your project and offers substantial money up front for exclusive rights, run away. Plant patents on attractive plants that catch the public's interest can make enormous profits for you if you retain your rights."

He glanced down fondly at the desk where his pink marigolds were sitting. "These, by the way, have been registered with the patent office and will be grown over the next two years before release to the public. I have contracts already signed with hundreds of nurseries and mail-order plant firms."

"In other words, you're going to get very, very rich?" Ursula piped up. "I hope you'll consider using some of the money for good causes. I could suggest some to you."

"Thank you, but I have good causes of my own," Dr. Eastman said stiffly. "As I was saying, five: A well-planned full-scale introduction of the plant to the public is the only way to go. Certain companies will act as agents for you on a sliding scale of royalties. The first year is the most expensive. As much as forty percent of your royalties on the plants shipped."

"Forty percent for an agent?" Stefan Eckert

exclaimed. "Golly! I'm writing a textbook on educational management and I'd heard that agents only charged ten to fifteen percent."

"I have no knowledge of literary agents," Dr. Eastman said as if he were proud of this fact. "As I was saying, six: You should know a lot about your triallers. They should have experience in the plant type, be known as efficient and prompt in reporting results, and have a solid reputation for keeping confidential testing quiet."

Only Stefan and old Arnold Waring were taking extensive notes of the lecture, but freshly pressed Charles Jones and his neighbor Miss Martha Winstead were paying very close attention and seemed extremely interested.

"Now we'll take a break for about five minutes, and come back and let Mrs. Nowack order us around and assign drivers and passengers." This might have been insulting, except that he said it with a sincere smile at Shelley. "And we'll be off then to see my garden and Mrs. Appledorn's."

"*Ms*. Appledorn, if you don't mind," Ursula said.

Nine

Shelley drove Jane and Miss Martha Winstead. "Do you know the way?" Miss Winstead asked.

"Approximately," Shelley said.

"I can show you the house."

68

"Oh . . . you knew Dr. Eastman before this class?" Jane asked.

Miss Winstead turned slightly in the front seat and said to Jane in the seat behind her, "All too well."

There wasn't time to question this remark before they arrived at a small white colonial home with clipped hedges and lush grass in the front yard, but no flowers at all.

"Isn't that odd," Jane said. "I'm seeing so many more front-yard gardens in the last few years. You'd think a professional in the field would have lots of gardens."

"It's a contagious thing," Miss Winstead said. "In the fifties and sixties you never saw gardens in front yards. Flowering shrubs like forsythia and dogwoods were barely acceptable. For some reason most homeowners thought gardens should be private. But when I put a garden along my driveway, the next year there were two small garden window boxes on either side of me, and some trees that had hostas and impatiens around them. The year after that, two of my neighbors made nice raised beds of begonias and dracaena. Now nearly every house on the block has something flowering in 'public,' so to speak. But there are still whole blocks where nobody has started the trend. Mrs. Jeffry, may I help you get out of the back of the vehicle?"

With Shelley at the wheel, Jane expected that they would be the first to arrive. But Dr. Eastman was already at home. He must be an even faster driver than Shelley. A horrifying thought.

"No, thanks," Jane said. "I'm getting the hang of it." She was afraid she'd fall out the door and crush Miss Winstead, though on second thought, Miss Winstead looked quite durable.

Dr. Eastman was standing at a gate at the side of the house to welcome the class, but didn't appear to notice Miss Winstead. Instead, he spoke pointedly to Jane and Shelley.

"Go right on back and take a look. This is, of course, only a part-time home for me and nothing like my house and garden upstate."

Jane was prepared to be disappointed after this warning. She hobbled down the side yard, which had a wooden fence with a few hanging pots of ivy and begonias. It was cool and dark and restful. Instead of a sidewalk, there was a wooden walkway with ferns here and there along the sides.

Nothing was spectacular, but the begonias were in full bloom and the ivy and ferns were spectacularly well kept. Not a spot or hint of yellowing on a single leaf. Entering the backyard behind Shelley and Miss Winstead, Jane was surprised. There were several large pines at the back of the lot where the yard sloped upward that were quite large and almost entirely concealed the house behind. In front of the pines were small islands of color and scattered, delicate-looking small plum trees. And there were quite a few Asian-looking ornaments.

But the garden was an exercise in restraint. Watching her step carefully, she limped along to a flagstone patio with a pair of old ceramic Foo dogs guarding the entrance. Shelley and Miss Winstead had abandoned her and were looking at something under the pines that appeared to be a sort of miniature teahouse.

The lawn was cool and green and so thick and evenly cut that it looked very like a fine carpet. The paths were made of tiny round stones embedded in a dark background that must have been dyed cement. Not the thing you'd want to walk on with crutches.

A Japanese woman came out the back door. "Hello," Jane said. "Dr. Eastman has invited the class to see his yard. Are you Mrs. Eastman?"

The woman's face crinkled into a smile. She pointed to herself and said, "Housekeeper. This my grandson, Joe."

A bright-eyed but serious-looking boy with black hair as tidy as the lawn had joined them. "Grandma has never learned much English, I'm afraid. What did you do to your leg, miss?"

Jane couldn't make up a lie to this nice, polite, solemn child. He looked about twelve years old—a very composed twelve-year-old. "I just fell off a curbing. It's a boring thing, but true."

"Would you like to walk about or take a chair?" he asked. His grandmother was standing behind him now, her hand on his shoulder, bobbing her head in a half-nodding, half-bowing manner.

"I'll walk about a bit, thank you," Jane said with the same formal tone.

She got her crutches lined up and started out to

follow Shelley around. Sensing movement behind her, she turned slightly. The boy was stooping along behind her and brushing up the round dents her crutches made in the grass.

"I'm so sorry," Jane said, "but I'm afraid to walk on the round stones."

"No problem, miss," he said. "Perhaps you'd be more comfortable sitting in the shade, however."

Jane reconsidered and took his advice. His grandmother rushed inside and got a very pretty embroidered pillow to put behind her back as she sat down on a teak bench. "Thank you so much," Jane said, and couldn't resist a little pleasant head bobbing in return.

The rest of the class followed quickly and all of them walked obediently along the stone paths, examining small sculptures and little mounds of subtly shaded flowers. Lavender and pale blue and light yellow mounds with perfect foliage. From Jane's vantage point she couldn't tell what they were.

"It's a very pretty yard, Joe. Do you help take care of it?"

"Yes, miss."

"You do a very good job."

"Thank you, miss."

Polite conversations with polite children were hard on Jane. She gazed about, murmuring things like, "Oh, how pretty the paths are" and "Isn't that a lovely flowering bush?"

The garden was too perfect for her taste. There

72

wasn't a thing wrong with it except its exactitude. Everything was precisely round, or oblong, or gently curved with great precision. There didn't appear to be a weed anywhere or a blade of grass out of place. Or a single object misplaced by an inch. It was soothingly bland. Nothing to excite or disturb the senses. She wondered whether this represented Dr. Eastman's taste or that of the housekeeper and her grandson.

Shelley and Miss Winstead wandered over to where Jane was sitting, and the housekeeper provided them with pillows as well. Her bobbing presence was daunting, but once the two chairs and bench were filled with sitters, she backed away and disappeared into the house. A moment later, she reappeared with an armload of fragile-looking folding chairs for the rest of the guests.

Joe was following Dr. Eastman and Stefan Eckert as they approached the tall, dense pines. Eastman pulled down a branch and was apparently telling Eckert something about it. Ursula was on her own, bending over to smell every clump of flowers. She was the only one with the nerve or insensitivity to actually touch any of the plants or ornaments. Arnold Waring was also on his own. Jane hadn't realized how barrel-chested the older man was until she saw him moving about. He carefully studied each area of the yard, as if mapping it in his mind.

When he got near Ursula, she all but grabbed him by the lapels to pontificate about something. He nodded several times and eased himself away from her, but she pursued him, still talking. Finally, in desperation, he simply turned his back on her and walked away.

Geneva Jackson, who hadn't been in the class this morning, had joined the group now, and she and the cardboard-stiff Charles Jones were chatting over a Hindu-type sitting stone figure.

"Julie Jackson must be getting better," Shelley said, "or Geneva wouldn't be here. I'll have a word with her."

Left alone with Miss Winstead, Jane asked, "How long have you known Dr. Eastman?"

"Since a year before he married my cousin Edwina."

"Oh, you're related then."

"Barely, I'm glad to say."

Jane was fascinated by these mysterious hints. "Miss Winstead, Shelley and I were talking about going to a late lunch together after the tour. Would you like to join us?"

"That would be lovely. You two young women seem to be old friends."

"We've lived next door to each other for twenty years."

"That surprises me. Someone told me you grew up in a diplomat's family. I thought you'd be used to moving from place to place."

She and Jane chatted a bit about Jane's childhood, and Miss Winstead contributed that her family had traveled to some of the same cities when she was young. By the time they'd exhausted the subject, the rest of the group had finished their tour of the yard and were moving toward the side yard where they'd entered.

Ursula was approaching Jane, who feared she was coming to help her or ask how she'd enjoyed her dinner last night. Jane fairly sprang to her feet and said to Miss Winstead that they'd better get a move on.

"Certainly," Miss Winstead said, with a knowing sparkle in her eyes.

Ten

Ursula's garden was next. Jane dreaded seeing it.

As they pulled up to Ursula's house, Jane was once again surprised. The front lawn was ratty, with some almost bare spots, but Jane's own front yard was nearly as bad. Her son Mike claimed it was because she'd overwatered and caused a fungus. He was bringing something home from the nursery to treat it. Maybe she'd share that information with Ursula. Or maybe she'd be better off keeping quiet. Ursula would probably see another dangerous conspiracy in chemical treatments of lawns.

The house itself wasn't too bad either, a single story that sprawled a bit. The greenhouse at the west end, which looked distinctly homemade with "found" materials, was something of a blight. But the house itself was painted a pale green with navy trim around the windows and doors and a deep magenta front door. A fairly popular color combination lately. The windowpanes themselves were dirty and streaked, the front door had a small hole in the screen, and the door itself showed dog scratches. But all in all, it wasn't the tumbledown hovel Jane had expected.

They arrived even before Ursula and waited in the minivan for the other car pools to arrive. "I've invited Miss Winstead to join us for lunch," Jane said to Shelley.

"I know, so did I," Shelley responded. "Where shall we go?"

By the time they'd settled on a restaurant, the rest of the group had pulled up and were getting out of their cars. Ursula was really excited and not even bothering to pick up the items that were falling out of her bags. Shelley picked up a handheld calculator and gave it back to her as they went around the side of the house. Miss Winstead rescued an invitation to some sort of community meeting and likewise returned it.

There was a big wooden door to the backyard that was a little crooked on its hinges, which Ursula had to struggle to open. "I don't usually come around this way. Sorry," she said. The door finally creaked back and she made a grand entry gesture that dislodged a butterfly hairpin, which Arnold Waring picked up, grunting with the effort of finding it under an overgrown spirea bush.

When they got to the backyard, there was a cacophony of barking from inside the house. Ursula opened the back door and shouted, *"QUIET!"* The barking subsided.

The "garden" was much like Jane imagined it would be. Completely wild and disorderly. Some flat rocks that looked suspiciously like tombstones lay about, forming rough paths. Somewhere genealogists were wondering where their great-great-aunt Mildred's final memorial had gone.

There was no grass at all, just a jumble of plants and trees and bushes. Mostly too dry. There were holes in the ground where apparently useless plants had been yanked out. And there was an overpowering smell of decay.

"That's the compost pile you smell," Ursula said proudly. "I'm surprised I didn't see one in your yard, Dr. Eastman. It's the heart of gardening."

"You just couldn't smell it," he said. "It's hidden behind the pines. And compost piles should never have an odor like this unless you're putting pet waste in it."

Jane wasn't going to risk breaking her other foot taking the full tour, and looked around for a place to sit down. There were two iron benches near the house, but they were white with bird droppings. There must have been about fourteen bird feeders hanging from the eaves. Most of them were empty or had an inch or two residue of mildewed seeds. Only the hummingbird feeder looked fresh, but it didn't have any customers. Jane propped her armpits on the crutches and looked around. She noticed that here and there, dusty electrical wires emerged from the ground and led into one of the areas. Probably some sort of lighting Ursula could turn on at night.

There were a few neat things in the garden when you studied it. A peculiar iron sculpture about four feet high that looked like a bunch of rusted airplane propellers gone awry caught her eye and whimsy.

A statue of a woman, nearly life-sized and graceful, was gently turning from copper to green. Morning glories had climbed her and wreathed her upturned head. Jane wondered if this was coincidental or a product of training them that way.

A stand of bachelor buttons in a deep, eye-watering blue stood solid and proud among a sprinkling of towering bright yellow cosmos with lovely ferny foliage. A tilted, broken wheelbarrow spilled out masses of pink geraniums.

It was, if nothing else, a messy garden with a lot of blighted areas among spots of true beauty.

She heard a little cough behind her and turned to see Charles Jones watching her. "Aren't you going to walk around and look?" she asked.

He shook his head. "I don't want to go home with ticks just to see a bunch of rubble."

"But sometimes rubble is good—in small doses. Look at that big piece of egg-and-dart molding among the pink petunias. That's a good combination," Jane persisted.

"It's okay, I guess. If you like that sort of clutter," he said, dismissing Jane's view.

Of course he would hate a garden like this, Jane thought. He was so tidy and crisp and somehow disgustingly clean. She assumed he was a bachelor who would consider sex to be messy and disorganized.

"Is it," she said, "that you dislike the garden, or Ursula, or both?"

"Both," he said without hesitation. "If I lived next door to this . . . mess, I'd complain to the city, put up a solid fence, or just move away. Gardens should be things of beauty and precision. Like Dr. Eastman's. Though I don't believe he is really the gardener there."

"Not high on the chaos theory, are you?" Jane said, trying to make it sound like a joke.

He just stared at her with confusion.

Shelley returned from her tour picking burrs off her slacks. "Interesting place," she said to Charles and Jane. "Can you see the waterfall from here?" She turned and peered back out into the yard. "No, I guess you can't. It's . . . interesting. A wall of clear violently colored marbles with tiny lights behind them here and there. The water absolutely shimmers over it. Ursula says she's done all this work entirely by herself."

"Obviously," Charles Jones said. If his face hadn't been so utterly bland, Jane would have sworn he was sneering.

The rest of the crowd was drifting back toward the patio. Geneva Jackson was smiling slightly, shaking her head in apparent disbelief. Stefan Eckert was trying to pull an especially clingy vine with thorns off his golf shirt. Arnold Waring simply looked stunned, and Miss Martha was grinning as she made scribbles in a notebook. Maybe she was the only one besides Jane who saw interesting things about Ursula's garden.

When everyone started thanking Ursula for the tour, however insincerely, she exclaimed, "Oh, but you haven't seen—or heard—everything yet. It's a proven fact that plants thrive on music. Wait here."

She dashed into the house, and a moment later, there was a blast of noise. Not music.

"I know it doesn't sound terribly nice together," Ursula said, reemerging from her house. She had to bellow to be heard. "But different plants need different kinds of music. Perennials, for the most part, prefer opera. I can't imagine why, but after long experimentation, I realized it's their favorite. The cornflowers and the hostas like marches. You wouldn't think they had that in common, would you? They're not the least like each other."

Everybody just gawked. Only Arnold Waring, holding a cupped hand behind his right ear, was making a serious polite effort to hear what she was saying.

"And the columbines love rock music," it sounded as if she was saying.

"We'll assemble in class tomorrow morning," Dr. Eastman screamed at the group, "and discuss hybridizing. Then go . . . . where, Mrs. Nowack?"

"To Miss Winstead's garden and Mr. Jones's," Shelley shouted, consulting her schedule.

As they escaped the noise and headed for the front yard, Ursula caught up with Jane. "Where are you off to?" Ursula asked.

Jane, who felt honor-bound to let the others go first

instead of having her hold them back, was ready with an invented errand. "Another meeting."

"All three of you?"

"It's a library thing," Miss Winstead, who was just in front of Jane, said over her shoulder. "And we're already late. Jane, get in the van so we can go. Ms. Appledorn, I've enjoyed your garden immensely. It's clear that you love it."

They sped off before Ursula could invite herself along, and left her smiling at them.

When they reached the Chinese restaurant they'd selected, a woman customer who was opening the door held it for Jane. "What did you do to yourself?" she asked, as Jane narrowly missed cracking the stranger's ankle with the left crutch.

"Just a hang-gliding accident," Jane said. "Bad landing, I'm afraid."

"How fascinating. You landed on your foot, I guess."

"No, actually a tree broke my fall, but I got the foot caught in a crotch of the tree and had to hang there upside down for ages before someone got me down."

"I can't wait to tell my husband this," the woman said. "He thinks hang gliding sounds like fun."

"Elephants, now hang gliding," Shelley muttered as they took a table.

"But she enjoyed the story," Jane said. "I hate to disappoint people."

Miss Martha smiled broadly. "I admire your imagination. How did you really do it?"

"Tripped over a curbing," Jane admitted. "At Julie Jackson's house."

"What were you doing there? Are you friends of hers?"

"We barely knew her," Shelley explained. "Some flowers for her were accidently delivered to Jane, who has the same address but a different street name, and we were taking them over to where they belonged."

They ordered their drinks and looked over the list of what was on today's buffet. Shelley asked Miss Winstead if she knew Julie Jackson.

"Not well," Miss Winstead said. "Years ago she occasionally did some research at the library, but most often, I suppose, she used the university facilities. I haven't laid eyes on her for years. Now research is at the tip of the fingers for anyone who knows how to search the Internet. Especially for scientific or government publications."

"What, exactly, is her job?" Shelley asked.

"She's a microbiologist, it says in the brochure for the class," Jane said. "Do either of you know what that is?"

Neither Shelley nor Miss Winstead could define the job.

"What did Geneva tell you about Ms. Jackson's condition?" Jane asked Shelley.

"Not much to report. Stable, but not improving noticeably."

"That sounds like a bad thing," Jane said. "If she

82

were going to improve, I'd think they'd see some progress by now."

Shelley shook her head. "Her sister said it was normal considering the blow. The brain just needs to rest awhile, she thinks. They've done all sorts of tests—X rays and sonograms and such—and there doesn't seem to be a blood clot or increased swelling. Geneva says this is a good sign."

"Miss Winstead . . . ?" Jane said hesitantly. "You seemed to be indicating earlier that you were related to Dr. Eastman and not happy about it. Would it be too nosy to ask why?"

"Not at all. I wouldn't have said anything if I considered it a secret. I knew him when we were both young and in college. We dated for a while, but it wasn't a match made in heaven, as they say. I was too smart and independent even then for him. But the last event we attended together was a big family dinner at my grandmother's. My cousin Edwina was there. People were always mistaking us for each other, we looked so much alike. Edwina was the dearest girl. Not quite as simple-minded as single-minded. She wanted nothing of life but to be a wife and mother. Not at all like me or young women today. Very old-fashioned."

"You were fond of her," Jane said.

"I was. I couldn't understand or agree with Edwina's thinking, but admired her sense of knowing her purpose in life. I was still trying to figure out whether I wanted to be Amelia Earhart or Eleanor Roosevelt or Joan of Arc. She was perfect for Stewart Eastman. We were both pretty girls, but he wanted a compliant, domestic wife, not a bright one. They were married a year after they met."

She paused and drew a breath. "Let's get our food and I'll tell you the rest while we eat, if you're interested." She scooted out of the booth and went to look over the food. Shelley handed Jane her crutches and said under her breath, "I don't think this is going to be a story of unrequited love. Come along and show me what you want and I'll fill your plate."

"Why? The plate, I mean."

"Have you not noticed yet that you have both hands busy with the crutches? Were you planning to walk around with the plate on your head?"

Eleven

The three women came back to the table with their first course of appetizers. Jane had loaded up on crab Rangoon, Shelley on egg rolls, and Miss Winstead on a single spring roll, which she ate with generous dollops of hot mustard that didn't even cause her eyes to water the slightest bit. The first time Jane had tried this restaurant's mustard, she'd wept, and choked, nearly fainted, and couldn't taste anything for three days afterward.

Since she was the first to finish, Miss Winstead went on with her story. "Edwina was the perfect wife for Stewart for a couple years. He wasn't the perfect husband, though. She desperately wanted children. He told her they couldn't afford to raise a family on his meager teaching salary while he was getting his advanced degrees. After four or five years, he had his doctorate and was near the top of his field.

"In the academic world, this meant lots of politicking. Buttering up his betters, entertaining lavishly, and intellectually shining. And Edwina ceased to be of any use to him. She didn't speak the same language as the faculty wives. Her interests were baking and cleaning, not social climbing and backbiting. She was sweet, but rather dim, I have to admit."

"Poor girl," Jane said. "How did she cope?"

"She didn't have to," Miss Winstead said with a catch in her voice. "I don't think she ever realized he considered her a liability instead of an asset. She became ill with ovarian cancer. A death sentence in those days. Stewart delivered the divorce papers to her while she was still dopey after the surgery."

Jane nearly spit out her food with outrage. *"NO!"*

Several other diners turned to look at them.

"Yes," Miss Winstead said softly. "She lasted only a week longer. She'd simply lost her entire will to live."

"How can you bear to be around the man?" Shelley asked.

"It's revenge, I'm afraid. I turn up every time he speaks anywhere in the area. I take notes and hunt down errors to correct the next time he speaks. I owe it to Edwina, poor dear girl, to avenge her. I remind him of her and his cruel treatment every time I show up. Merely by showing up. You must think I'm a real old harridan."

"Not at all. If something like that happened to someone I loved, I'd hope I have the wit and ability to remind them for the rest of their miserable life," Shelley said passionately.

Miss Winstead brightened up and said, "Let's get the rest of our food."

When they were seated again, Shelley asked, "Do you know about the others in the class as well?"

"Some of them. Librarians often see only one side of patrons. The side that shows their private interests or their business needs. Ursula Appledorn is a frequent visitor. She apparently doesn't have a very good computer at home, or doesn't want to pay for a provider. She comes to the library to use ours and prints a lot of stuff out. Overall, it's more expensive for her to do it that way."

"Conspiracy stuff?" Jane asked. "Has she told you about the Denver airport?"

"Endlessly," Miss Winstead said. "It's her favorite one. The actual books she takes out on loan are usually about herbal cures, gardening, or dogs, and for fiction, she reads romances."

"Romances? That doesn't seem in character, somehow."

Miss Winstead shrugged. "Few people are really as one-sided as you think on slight acquaintance, I guess."

"What does she live on?" Shelley asked. "Does she have a job?"

"I have no idea," Miss Winstead said.

"Maybe she still baby-sits the elderly," Jane contributed. "And she said something about one of her old ladies leaving her a legacy. Maybe it was a really big one."

"What about Arnold Waring?" Shelley moved down the list.

"I don't know much about him. His wife was a dear, helpless little woman who came to the library at least once a week. She read practically every mystery story that came in. She especially liked anything to do with firefighters."

"Why?"

"Her husband had been one before he retired. They had no children, she said, and really appeared to live for each other. He'd drive her every week, would carry her books she was returning, and stand by the door to wait, and carry the new ones out. As if she were a delicate flower who couldn't carry them herself. It really was nice. Such a surly-looking, hulking man, taking such good care of his wife."

"When did she die? He mentioned her in class in the past tense," Jane said.

Miss Winstead thought for a while. "Maybe five years ago. Possibly four. I imagine he was devastated."

"And Stefan Eckert?" Jane asked.

"I know very little about him, although we've worked together over the years. He's an assistant to the man who runs the community relations at the junior college, and always full of ideas to pull the public into taking an interest and supporting the school. He often consults with me when he bags a big name, so the library can get the author's books in before the activity."

Jane said, "He told us he was the head of community relations."

"Wishful thinking, perhaps," Miss Winstead said.

"You sound a bit like you're damning with faint praise," Shelley said.

"I must be more transparent than I thought," Miss Winstead said with a chagrined smile. "Stefan's charming, but can be a bit aggressive about soliciting funds and grants. But he gets speakers for next to nothing that other, richer schools can't get to speak. I shouldn't say this, but I don't think Stefan is above a couple little white lies if it suits his aim. Ms. Jackson was one of the speakers he got, and I've tried to get her to speak at the library many times and she always said she didn't feel comfortable giving talks. But he got around her somehow. It's a pity she was injured. I was looking forward to hearing about her job."

"Do you know anything about Julie Jackson's life?" Jane asked.

"I see notices in the paper about high-society fund-raising parties, and she is always there on the arm of some rich, eligible man. Always a different one. I suppose it's because it's the 'done thing' in those circles to have an escort."

"Do you know anything about the investigation of the attack on her?" Shelley asked.

"Not a thing. It seems to me an example of a random act of violence."

Jane and Shelley exchanged looks. When Jane nodded, Shelley said, "I'm not sure how much you know about the attack. There are aspects of it that weren't in the papers. The person who attacked her came through the house, where there were plenty of things to steal, but took nothing, and went straight to the basement she had set up as an office."

Miss Winstead thought this over and said, "That's very peculiar, isn't it? If it was a robbery, why go straight to the basement? Did she have a safe or something down there that a repair person might know about?"

"We don't know," Jane said. "But the man I date is the investigating officer and he didn't mention a safe. I would think if there was one, he would probably have mentioned it."

Miss Winstead frowned for a long moment, then said, "You don't think . . . No, of course not . . ."

"What?" Jane and Shelley said in unison.

"No, it's absurd. But I just wondered if it might have anything to do with her being scheduled to teach this class."

"How could it?" Shelley asked.

Miss Winstead shrugged elegantly. "I don't know. It just popped into my mind because you were asking me about the people in the class."

Jane and Shelley both looked stunned. "I suppose in the back of my mind, I *was* thinking that," Jane admitted. "For no good reason except it happened so close to her giving a talk to this group."

"You think she might be in a position to reveal something about one of them?" Shelley asked.

Jane said, "Maybe. But what could that be? And why wouldn't she sort it out with the person in private instead of in front of witnesses? No, I don't think that would fly."

"But none of us know her personally," Miss Winstead said primly. "I think it's rash to make assumptions. It just as well could be that one of the escorts took himself too seriously, and she rejected him. A crime of passion that has nothing to do with her job."

The younger women felt like they'd been put in their place, and Jane reverted to what little she knew of the investigation. "Mel, that's the man I know who's the investigating detective, says it was a violent attack, and appeared that the attacker might not have expected her to be there."

"How on earth did he come to that conclusion?" Miss Winstead said with an air of criticism.

"Only because Geneva Jackson left the house with her husband earlier. The sisters look so much alike that the attacker, if he was watching the house, could have mistaken Geneva for Julie. It's only one theory," Jane said, feeling she had to defend Mel's thinking now that she had stupidly given away something she shouldn't have.

Miss Winstead nodded. "I suppose that does make sense. Who reported the attack?"

"I assume Geneva or her husband," Jane said. "They came home and found her injured, I suppose. They were at the house, anyway, when we got there with the misdirected flower arrangement."

"Jane, would you let me know what you learn of the investigation?" Miss Winstead asked.

That put Jane on the spot. She was already feeling like she'd dishonored Mel's confidences and shouldn't say any more.

"I doubt I'll be told any more about the investigation," she fudged. "Mel only mentioned the one idea because he was visiting me a couple hours later to see how badly I'd hurt my foot. Sort of thinking out loud, you know."

"I understand," Miss Winstead said rather formally. Jane was afraid the older woman understood all too well and was insulted.

The moment passed quickly, however, as there was a sudden bolt of lightning and the sound of a hard rain coming down on the roof of the restaurant.

"Nobody predicted this," Shelley said as she pulled aside the little curtain in the booth. "Wow, a real gully washer. I guess we're stuck here for a bit. Does it seem to you that the more technology the weather forecasters get, the more inaccurate they are? It used to be that the weather guy would go out on the roof of the studio and look at the sky and take a guess, and was right half of the time. Now they're wrong most of the time."

They spent the rest of the brief storm happily deriding local newscasters who had no training in speaking good English. A subject dear to Miss Winstead's heart. "They think notoriety and fame mean the same thing. I've heard so many grammatical errors that make me cringe."

"The other day, in the chat segment, one of them said, 'Me and my wife are going on vacation next week,'" Jane put in.

Miss Winstead shook her head sadly. "How utterly ignorant!"

Jane was glad the subject of Dr. Julie Jackson and the attack on her had been thoroughly squashed and forgotten.

But she couldn't stop herself from wondering why Miss Winstead had been eager enough to know about the investigation to ask Jane to share Mel's progress. Jane watched as the rain diminished and chided herself for being so suspicious.

Twelve

Jane was worn out from the morning and half the afternoon of traipsing around. She let herself down on the sofa and gently toppled sideways.

"Anything you need?" Shelley asked.

"Something really boring to read, so it puts me out."

Shelley went to the bookshelves and got down a gigantic paperback. "How about *The Arms of Krupp*?"

"I hate to admit I liked it," Jane said. "I read it the year Todd went to kindergarten and I finally had a whole three hours a day without kids around. I'll try it again."

"I'm starting a roast for you," Shelley said. "Don't worry, I'll be quiet." She went across the driveway to her house, got the roast, and came back. Quietly removing a pan from the cabinet, a cooking bag with seasonings, and a bit of water, she got it in Jane's oven with hardly a sound.

Tiptoeing back to the living room, she saw that Jane was sound asleep with the book open on her chest. There was a sound in the kitchen and Shelley whirled and scurried to the door. Mike had already opened it and was dripping wet.

"Shhh, your mom's sleeping. What happened to you?"

"A downpour at the nursery. They sent most of the clerks home because the forecast is for more rain. I've got to get dry clothes."

It wasn't until he moved away that Shelley realized that Kipsy had been standing behind him. "I'll bet you're Kipsy, right?" she said. "I was just starting a roast for the Jeffrys' dinner. Sit down and have a soft drink with me while Mike's upstairs. I'm Mrs. Nowack from next door."

"Hi, Mrs. Nowack. Mike's told me about you."

"All good things, I'm sure," Shelley said with a smile.

"Oh, yeah . . ."

"Kipsy, I've been wanting to have a little chat with you. If you don't mind."

"No, I guess not," Kipsy said, brushing some of the violently red bangs out of her face and taking a sip of the drink Shelley had poured.

"I have a question for you. You must go to a lot of trouble to look as you do. And I can't help but wonder why."

Kipsy started to stand up in preparation for stomping out.

Shelley put a hand on her arm. "I meant no criticism at all. I'm genuinely interested. I love to know about human nature."

Sullenly Kipsy lowered herself back onto the kitchen chair. "Yeah, me too."

"Didn't all those things you've had pierced hurt a lot?" Shelley asked.

"Not that much. They sorta numb you with a piece of ice."

"And it doesn't hurt to wear them either?"

"Uh-uh. Not often. The eyebrow ring sometimes gets stuck in my bangs, though, and it can be a bitch—I mean a pain to get it loose."

Shelley smiled supportively. "How interesting. I wonder, are you planning any changes in your appearance?"

"I was thinking about another tattoo, but can't think where to put it."

"The holes you've punched in yourself would probably close up if you changed your jewelry style, right?"

"I guess so," she said in a surly manner.

"But a tattoo is pretty much forever?"

"Why do you ask?"

"Let me ask my earlier question in another way. Are you planning to look this way when you're thirty or forty and even fifty?"

"Fifty!" Kipsy yelped. "I'll never be fifty."

Shelley shook her head. "But you will, you know. How will you feel about the tattoos then?"

Kipsy shrugged. "They'll have some way to get rid of them by that time. Laser stuff or something."

"So you imagine you'll want to get rid of them someday?"

"I hadn't thought about it."

"Do."

Shelley topped up Kipsy's drink. "You're probably a pretty girl. I want to understand what you mean people to think of you. Do you want to frighten them, or make them laugh, or think you're really cool and modern?"

"I don't think about that stuff. Mrs. Nowack, I can look any way I want. If my own mom doesn't care, why should you?"

Because I'm a better mother than yours, Shelley thought.

"I guess it's just because I am a mother," Shelley said offhandedly. "My daughter's a little younger than you and, of course, won't talk about her feelings with me. I'll bet you didn't talk to your mother when you were sixteen either. So partly, I want to know what to say if she wants to get a tattoo or to pierce her nose."

Kipsy mumbled something into her drink. Then looked defiantly at Shelley. "Tell her not to. Some of the kids laugh at me. I don't care. They're dummies. They're just scared of being themselves like I am. They're the insecure ones."

So somebody's called you insecure, Shelley thought. "Mike doesn't laugh at you, does he?"

"No, I guess he doesn't. He can see who I really am."

"I think I understand what you mean," Shelley said. She could hear Mike coming down the steps. "Thank you, Kipsy, for being honest with me." *And a tiny bit honest with yourself,* she added mentally.

"Are you two chewing the fat?" Mike said with a laugh. "That's something Grumps always says. Grumps is my grandpa," he explained to Kipsy. "But he's not grumpy at all. Let's go to a movie, since I have the rest of the afternoon off."

Kipsy got up and followed him to the door, but stopped and looked back for a moment at Shelley. "Thank you, too, Mrs. Nowack," she said.

Jane clumped into the kitchen a few minutes later. "You really put that girl through the wringer."

"I didn't mean to. It just perpetually perplexes me that kids will go out of their way to look foolish or dirty or bizarre. I must have missed that stage."

"Most of us do," Jane said, sitting where Kipsy had sat.

"But isn't it human nature to want to be liked?"

Jane tilted her head and considered. "Maybe not so

96

much liked as admired, I suppose. And sometimes feared. You scare the devil out of a lot of people, and I know perfectly well you enjoy it."

Shelley started to object, then grinned. "Only if they're jerks."

"So did you get a blinding insight from Kipsy?"

Shelley made a so-so motion with her hand. "I think no one had ever asked her why she wanted to look like a freak. I didn't say that outright—"

"I know. I was eavesdropping."

"I suspect she just needed parental guidance."

"You and I both know how well *that* goes over with teenagers."

"But they need it, even though they'd never in the world admit it. Teenagers love a good fight, especially when it has to do with their taste or friends or appearance. This poor Kipsy only got slightly haughty twice. That's a very low average."

"You're a stranger to her. And you can be scary."

"Only when I'm trying," Shelley said. "But as for being a stranger, all the more reason she was entitled to be rude to me. But she wasn't. You know, I think it's possible her mother doesn't really care what she does or how she looks. So she tries a little tattoo. Mom doesn't say anything. So then she pierces her nose and Mom doesn't notice. So she dyes her hair a perfectly awful color—"

"Are you really trying to figure her out? She might have a devoted mother who cries herself to sleep for failing with this girl. The mother might have other daughters who are model kids and can't figure out where Kipsy went wrong."

Shelley considered this. "You could be right."

"Say that again," Jane said, pretending to swoon. "I hear it so seldom. That roast is sure smelling great. Can you stay and eat it with us?"

"I wish I could. Paul's sister Constanza is coming to dinner."

Jane made an X in the air with her fingers. "Too bad. Has she searched your house lately?"

"Not that I know of. But she's gone to some diet that involves a lot of sprouts and pasta, and the only meat she can eat is veal and chicken. Skinned and broiled without fat."

"Last month it was only tofu and veggies, wasn't it? Speaking of which, what did you think of Ursula's garden?" Jane asked.

"I hate to admit this, but there were things I liked. If the marble fountain had been clear blue marbles instead of garish colors and maybe foil behind it, it would have been a knockout. I've been thinking of trying to find someone to make me one."

"Wish I'd seen it. I liked the statues. Especially the elegant lady in copper. And I think Miss Winstead admired some of the yard herself. I saw her taking notes."

"You seemed uneasy with Miss Winstead toward the end of lunch," Shelley said.

"I'd said too much of what Mel told us. I felt guilty about shooting off my mouth. Then a little alarmed when she wanted me to keep her up on what other theories he was coming up with."

"That was peculiar of her, come to think of it. And so was her opinion that we thought Ms. Jackson's attacker was someone in the class."

Jane was silent for a long moment. "But—what if it was?"

Thirteen

"Why would it make any sense that the attacker was one of the class?" Shelley asked.

She and Jane were getting hungry smelling the roast cooking and had gone outside to sit on Jane's patio. The heavy rains predicted for the rest of the day had stopped and it was cool and damp and reasonably comfortable outdoors.

"It could be one of them, I guess," Jane said, looking sadly at her backyard. Max and Meow were sitting side by side, studying the field behind the house for signs of movement. If another developer built houses there instead of going bankrupt before even starting, the cats would be bereft. The grass needed mowing, and there was a permanent path in a semicircle where Willard had been running back and forth for years from gate to gate, barking his fool head off at the mailman. There were even some dead leaves of tulips Jane had never gotten around to gathering up and disposing of. Her yard was really a disgrace.

"But it could be anyone else as well," Shelley argued. "Someone in her family, her profession, maybe a neighbor she'd had a falling-out with. For that matter, it could be a complete stranger, or a drug-crazed lunatic who was randomly testing back doors for one that was open."

"The lunatic would have stolen what was on the ground floor and fled," Jane said.

"Maybe or maybe not," Shelley argued, mainly for the purpose of arguing. "If he heard somebody moving around in the basement, he might have gone straight down and attacked Ms. Jackson for no reason whatsoever. Someone seriously into drugs might have thought that was a good idea."

"I suppose with enough drugs, anybody might think anything is a good idea," Jane responded, but wasn't considering the theory seriously and she doubted Shelley was either.

Shelley said, "What if it was Dr. Eastman who attacked her?"

Jane turned to look at her. "What would be the point of that?"

Shelley shrugged. "His name just came to mind because he's the instructor who replaced her. Maybe he has a crazy need to publicize himself and his marigolds."

Jane replied, "I'm sure he, like Julie, is asked to give a lot of talks to groups. Probably more than he wants to do. And the marigolds aren't even on sale for a couple more years, he said."

"I was thinking about what Miss Winstead said about him."

Jane thought a moment. "Do you suppose her version is the whole truth?"

"I wondered that as well," Shelley admitted. "But Eastman is obviously a man determined to get ahead. Promote himself. Make lots of money. Maybe what he really wants is fame."

"He is a difficult man to like. But I don't think any of these theories hold water."

Shifting gears, Shelley asked, "Mel hasn't been around much, has he?"

"He's busy with three different cases at once," Jane said. "He's been calling me at intervals, but I haven't actually laid eyes on him for a couple days."

"Has he told you anything more about Julie Jackson?"

"He's being silent as the grave about it. Says things are coming along in the investigation."

Shelley took a sip of her iced tea she'd brought along in a big, remarkably ugly purple plastic carafe. "Doesn't want us meddling in a neighborhood crime?"

Jane nodded. "I guess so. But we've been so much help to him before, you'd think he'd appreciate our skills," she said with a wry smile.

The door of a vehicle slammed in Shelley's driveway and she got up, saying, "Just a minute. I'll be back."

It was actually fifteen minutes before Shelley got back, saying, "That was the garden place."

"What garden place?"

"The one where your Mike works. I called them out to spruce up my yard."

"Shelley!" Jane exclaimed. "That's cheating! The class is coming to our yards the same day. You're going to show off and make me look even worse."

"You could have thought of it," Shelley said calmly. "Come see what they've done."

The formerly rather bland backyard had two young men mowing and using a Weed Eater around the edges of the lawn. A multitude of gorgeous plants in planters of every variety were sitting around the edge of the patio. A replica of an old-fashioned wooden wheelbarrow was full of yellow nasturtiums; a large watering can spilled out purple petunias. There was a cupid statue surrounded by little pots of lobelia, and about ten of those fake pottery pots that look real were scattered artfully about. From one pot sprouted a trellis covered with a coral wild rose. Tall spikes of veronica were next to the rose, and there was a huge pot of dark red sunflowers the color of good burgundy. Verbena was tucked in between, filling the gaps between the large pots.

Jane gaped at the transformation. "You—you! You don't even know what most of this is. How are you going to take care of this?"

"Easy. I just water for a couple days and when the garden tour is over, these nice boys come back and take it all away."

"You *RENTED* a garden?"

"Why not? It wasn't all that expensive. And it was

102

easy. One plant catalog and one phone call."

Jane glared at her friend. "I was just going to send Mike out with the pooper-scooper and a lawn mower the night before, and keep the cats inside so they didn't leave mangled chipmunks on the patio. I even considered getting a tablecloth for the patio table and a little arrangement of flowers from the grocery store. And you go and re-create the Biltmore gardens for yourself. I call that cheating. I really do."

Shelley brushed this insult off. "As I say, anyone could have thought of it."

Jane made a raspberry noise.

"Mrs. Nowack," one of the workers asked, "do you want your shrubs trimmed?"

Shelley made a flighty gesture and said, "Yes. Soldier on, my good man."

Jane clumped home and took another critical look at her yard, noting the bug-chewed white petunias in the south corner, the straggling butterfly bush that had never bloomed, the stingy little marigolds. Then she went inside and called the nursery where Mike worked. Maybe since she was the mother of an employee, they'd give her a discount.

She was hardly off the phone when, a moment later, the doorbell rang. It was Arnold Waring holding a square pan with foil over it.

"Come in . . . Arnie," Jane said, remembering that he'd asked the class to call him that.

"Ms. Appledorn was telling me today about the awful food she brought you." He paused. "I hope you didn't like it, but maybe it *was* to your taste."

"Not my taste at all. I threw it all away. Though she meant well."

He looked relieved to hear this. "Well, I got home and took to thinking that it might be nice to have something better around. These are brownies from my wife's recipe file. Where would you like me to put them?"

"You made them yourself?" Jane said, leading him to the kitchen and indicating the counter.

"Oh, Miss Jeffry, I have to cook for myself. Never cooked for one person until Darlene passed on. But I used to cook for a gang at the fire station before I retired. At least twice a week now, I go to Darlene's little recipe box. She was such a good cook. It makes me feel—well, a little bit as if she's still with me. In spirit, anyway."

"That's sweet of you," Jane said. "I'm sure she knows you're doing that and is pleased."

Suddenly he was bustling back to the front door. Speaking over his shoulder, he said, "Mustn't keep you. Just thought you might like the brownies."

Jane followed him, thanking him, but he was gone.

Jane and her daughter were finishing a late dinner. Mike hadn't returned and Jane was wondering wildly if Mike and Kipsy had eloped. He was usually very good at letting his mother know where he was. Well . . . he was that way when he was in high school. A year of college had apparently put this courtesy out of his mind.

Ursula had called and said she was on the way with more food, and Jane said she was already putting her dinner on the table, and Ursula believed it even though it was only four-thirty when she called.

Katie was still speaking with a fake French accent, and Jane pretended not to notice. "The French, they would never use a plastic bag to cook meat. They use fine parchment paper," Katie commented.

"All of them?" Jane said sarcastically. "Katie, you were only in Paris with rich friends. And I doubt you got to go in the kitchen of the restaurants."

"But we did." Katie reverted momentarily to plain English. "Jenny's dad had gone to culinary school when he was young, and he always asked to see the kitchen before we ordered."

Jane was appalled. "Jenny's dad is a banker. Culinary was twenty years in his past, and I remember him telling me it made him gain weight and he quit after the first year and took business courses. And what's more, 'nice' people from America don't insist on seeing the kitchens of restaurants. It's a wonder you weren't all thrown out."

The argument was put on hold when Mel rang the front doorbell. Katie flounced to the hall and let him in, saying in bored tones, "She's in the kitchen criticizing my friends." She continued the flounce clear upstairs where she turned her radio on full blast.

Mel came in the kitchen smiling. "Who are you raking over the coals now?"

"No one you know," Jane said with a grin. "Sit down.

There are tons of leftovers. I'll bet you haven't had dinner."

"Or lunch for that matter. Thanks."

Jane had learned early on that you didn't try to talk to Mel when he was hungry. If he answered at all, it was merely "uh-huh" or "no." But she was anxious to pick his mind about Julie Jackson. She sat patiently as he ate four slices of the roast, and two helpings of potatoes and gravy, and passed on the broccoli au gratin.

While he was making inroads on the leftovers, she told him about Shelley renting plants. "It wasn't fair. Our yards are on the same day and it would make me look like a piker."

"But you've got more sense than to do a silly thing like that," he managed to say between bites.

"Not exactly . . ." Jane said softly. "Mine are coming tomorrow afternoon. And I even got a water feature to one-up her. It's only a little birdbath waterfall that I wanted anyway and actually bought outright."

"Is it the broken foot that's making you so competitive? Or something else?" Mel asked, setting down his silverware at last and really looking at Jane.

She looked at him for a long time. "It's more. And stupider. See, I've never broken any bone. It makes me feel as if I'm suddenly vulnerable and—well, getting older."

"But you might as well have broken your foot when you were eight or nine and you wouldn't have felt that way. I broke my arm about that age, and I thought it was sort of neat and made me stand out in the crowd, as I remember. Everybody breaks something, some-time. You've just been lucky."

"Yes, but there's a difference between eight and forty-something. And it reminds me, too, that I'm older than you."

Mel looked genuinely stunned. "When has that *ever* mattered? It's only a couple of years and you've aged far better than I have."

Jane got teary and reached across the table, putting her hands to his cheeks. "I sometimes forget what a good man you are."

Mel took one of her hands and kissed the palm, grinning. "You just want to pry information out of me, don't you?"

"NO! I wasn't even thinking of that. But now that you mention it—"

"Let's go sit in the living room where you'd be more comfortable, then."

When Mel had gallantly seated Jane and put sofa pillows behind her back and was assured she was comfortable, he sat down and took her plastered leg on his lap and said, "Frankly, we're getting nowhere fast with the Jackson case. Too many suspects, too little evidence."

"What suspects?" Jane asked, glancing around for something long she could stick down her cast to scratch an itch on the back of her leg. She settled on an emery board she found in the side table.

"Lots of men. Dr. Jackson was quite the socialite. She'd married young, twice in a row, then went off men as marriage partners, apparently. But she had quite a social life. She was on all sorts of high-tone charity boards and went to lots of fancy dinners. Always with an escort. Her bankbook and closet are both things you'd envy. Lots of money and lots of very elegant clothes." He took the emery board away from her. "You don't want to do that."

"What about the ex-husbands?"

"No go. One was at a business meeting in Hong Kong and the other was on vacation with his third wife and four children in Martha's Vineyard. Lots of creditable witnesses. And both exes expressed what sounded like genuine sorrow that she'd been injured and asked if there was anything they could do for her."

"What about the other men? The ones that wine and dine her at the charity dinners?"

"It's quite a list. And they're all successful men who are at the top of their fields and know how to keep their heads when questioned by the police. They all also expressed their concern and sounded quite sincere. Her hospital room would be crammed with flowers and fruit baskets if they were allowed in the intensive care area."

Jane brushed this off. "Any of them have alibis?"

"Some have good ones, a few have none. But that doesn't mean much. Lots of those sorts of executives work from home these days, at least part of the time, and since many of them are single or divorced, there's nobody to alibi them, and it doesn't make them guilty of anything."

"How is Julie doing, really?"

"She's coming around pretty well. Her brother-in-law says it's amazing that she was semiconscious for so long and there doesn't seem to be any permanent brain damage. She's pretty alert now."

"What has she to say about what happened to her?"

Just then the phone rang. "Want me to get it?" Mel asked. "It could be for me."

"Please, and if it's Mike, I want to talk to him."

Mel picked up the phone and said, "VanDyne here." Then, "Yes, I am . . . yes, she's fine. She finished her dinner . . . Tofu? I don't think so."

He came back shaking his head. "It was an Ursula asking if you'd finished the tofu. Who on earth is Ursula? And why would you eat tofu?"

Fourteen

"I'll tell you about Ursula later. Go back to where we were. If Julie's so alert, what is she telling you about the perp and what happened?"

"Absolutely nothing. She can't remember anything beyond having steak on the grill with her sister and sister's husband the night before she was attacked."

"But she will, though, sooner or later," Jane said.

Mel shook his head. "Her brother-in-law says in a serious accident, the immediate memory of it sometimes never comes back. He explained it's natural for the brain to file it away somewhere literally unreachable. A self-defense fear mechanism, if I understood him. Sort of a self-hypnotism for protection from the memory."

"Couldn't she be hypnotized for real when she recovers?"

Mel had sat back down and was idly tapping his fingers on her cast. "Only if she would agree to it. And it might be something she can't bear to remember, or perhaps she can't be hypnotized. Some people can't, you know. And anyway, she'll have a pretty long recovery time. She's got a touch of amnesia about other things as well. The neurologist thinks the non-threatening memories will return pretty fast."

"I guess you've taken fingerprints from her office?"

Mel raised his eyebrows and said, "You doubted that? Of course we did. But most of her files seem to have been handled by other people somewhere along the line. Lots of prints, but none matching her sister or her brother-in-law except on innocuous personal letters. And even the letters were filed in the color-coded booklets."

"So you suspect her sister or brother-in-law?"

"It's routine to suspect family members, Jane. Most violent crimes are within the family."

"Do you still think either one of them could have done it?"

Mel shook his head. "The sister had time-stamped receipts from her shopping that matched the tags on the clothes she'd bought. Her husband had a parking ticket at a garage in Chicago that covered most of the time they say they were gone, allowing for the travel back and forth."

"Does that let them off the hook?"

"Not necessarily. The time of the attack is hard to guess, so in theory they could have roughed her up before they left her house. We have only their word that she was all right when they left. Too bad the perp didn't break her watch in the attack, so we could tell when it happened. Unfortunately, that only happens in books."

"What about her files? Could you tell if anything was missing?"

"Two of the file drawers were gaping open. She might have left them that way while she was working. There isn't any huge gap and nothing's strewn around."

"Computer?"

"It's being gone over. There doesn't seem to be anything so far that indicates recent threats or personal conflicts."

"Is there something older in the files that does indicate conflicts?"

"Much older. Most of her files are letters outlining the plants she's been asked to analyze. All sorts of stuff about DNA and cell structure of the various parts of the plant, a full description, and pictures someone's provided are in each file as well. And the receipts for her work. A few people argued about her results, but fairly mildly."

"Does this have to do with disputed plant patents?"

Jane said, remembering something Dr. Eastman had said in class.

"Only a very few. Most seem to be from people who intend to apply for a patent and want to double-check if their submission is too much like anything she's studied before. I'm told by an expert in the patent outfit that this happens often because getting the patent is so expensive that people often would rather pay an outside expert before submitting the patent information. Her sister said it's been a couple of years at least since she had to testify in court about a disputed patent. The rest of the time, she writes articles for botany texts and specialty magazines."

"Was there a file from Dr. Stewart Eastman?"

"Who's that?"

"The guy with the pink marigolds he's patenting. Also the man who took over teaching the class when Julie couldn't do it."

"Doesn't ring a bell, but I'll check. Pink marigolds? Is that possible?"

"It seems so," Jane said. "He brought them to class to show off."

Mel went to the phone and gave Eastman's name to someone in his office who had a list of Julie's files. Waited a long time, then said, "Thanks."

While he was gone, Jane recovered the emery board and had a good, long, satisfying scratching session. She slipped it into the sofa cushions as he returned.

"No, Jane, no Eastman in the files. Why would you think he might be involved?"

"I don't really. It's just that he patents plants, and seemed to know Julie and her sister."

"What class is this anyway?"

"It was supposed to be basic botany. Shelley and I signed up just hoping to learn what kind of plants might grow for us. It turned out that Eastman's interest is entirely in patenting plants, not the basics like we expected. It's sort of interesting in theory, but not something of practical value to anyone in the class."

"And is this where the strange Ursula comes into your life? Who in the world is she?" Mel asked.

Jane sighed. "Ursula is hard to describe. She's an aging hippy. All tie-dyed and madly liberal or maybe madly conservative. I haven't quite figured that out. And she thinks there are vast conspiracies everywhere."

"What does this have to do with tofu?" Mel asked, laughing.

"She says she was a nurse in Vietnam and has taken care of a lot of old ladies since she lost her nursing status. She admitted it was a drug charge, but denies that it was valid. Only herbal cures. And free-range eggs and health food."

Mel had stopped laughing. "Oh, right. I better check her out."

"Can you do that?"

"I hope so. But why is she calling you?"

Jane smiled. "Because she's got me marked as helpless—like the old ladies. And she must not have an old lady currently to look after. You should have *seen* the food she brought over. Tofu was the least disgusting. Mel, I think she means well, but she sort of scares me."

"In what way?"

"I guess it's the conspiracy thing. She talks about it all the time. The government is trying to poison us with strawberries, the Denver airport is really owned by Queen Elizabeth, and the Masons control the world, the postal service in particular. It's just all so bizarre and paranoid. And even the so-called facts she cites are entirely wrong, but she doesn't want to know that."

"Facts like what?" Mel asked.

"Are you really interested? Let me think. She had the Templars a century off and seemed to think the Dauphin had survived and was English and formed the Virginia Company, which, if my memory for history is right, was long before he was even born."

"You're making this up."

Jane looked indignant. "I haven't the imagination to make up someone like Ursula. And if I could, I wouldn't."

"Who else is in this class? Is it a big group?"

"It might have been originally. It was scheduled in a large room," Jane said. "But the attack on Julie was in the local paper and maybe a lot of attendees assumed the class was canceled. You could ask Stefan Eckert about that."

"Who's he?"

"The junior college staff person who's in charge of community relations and set these summer classes up.

Well, he may be only second in charge. That's what Miss Winstead said."

"And is this Stefan odd, too?"

"Not at all. I think he got the job because he is so cheerful and handsome, though Miss Winstead hinted that he's up to something."

Mel got up and paced. "And Miss Winstead is . . . ?"

"Another person in the class. Former librarian. And former cousin-in-law of the substitute teacher, Dr. Eastman. She hates him."

"Why does she go to the class then?"

"You'll have to ask her the whole story, if you really want to know." Jane stopped and thought a minute. "That's odd . . . She'd signed up for the class to hear Julie speak, but said she always went to Eastman's lectures to make him uncomfortable. How would she have known he'd fill in?"

"If she knows the Stefan guy, he might have told her," Mel guessed.

Jane looked relieved. "That must be it. I'd hate to suspect Miss Winstead of anything worse than wanting to make a man she doesn't like miserable."

Mel was quiet for some time. Then he asked, "Do you really think anyone in the class *is* a suspect?"

Jane shrugged. "Probably not. I keep wavering. But since you have so many others to consider, I doubt it."

"Could you give me a list of the others in the group?" Mel pulled a notepad out of his jacket. "Stewart Eastman, Ursula Who?"

"Appledorn."

115

"And how do you spell the Stefan guy's name?"

"No idea," Jane replied. "But Miss Winstead is Martha. And she's a next-door neighbor of an obsessively tidy youngish man named Charles Jones. And there's an older man named Arnie Waring who used to be a firefighter. Shelley has everyone's addresses, since she made up the schedule for visiting the gardens."

"Anyone else?"

"Just Shelley and me. Are you going to investigate us?"

"I already have," Mel said with a straight face.

Jane laughed, then realized he was serious. "Did you really?"

"It was a long time ago. That cleaning-lady business. When she was strangled in Shelley's guest room. I didn't even know you then, except that you were there when I arrived."

And solved the case, Jane thought, but didn't say.

"Oh, I forgot. Geneva Jackson has come along to the classes, too. She says her husband sent her away from the hospital because she was getting on everyone's nerves because she's such a chirpy visitor."

"Was she signed up?"

"I don't think so. She's just stuck here until her sister is well, and apparently needed to fill her time with something interesting. She's involved in the plant business as well. You don't seriously think anyone in the class is responsible, do you?"

"Probably not, but it's interesting and might be relevant down the line. Jane, I'm falling-down tired. I better go home and get some sleep before something else comes up. Do you need anything done before I go?"

"Just one thing. Tell me what you thought when you met me the first time."

Mel grinned. "That you had terrific tits."

He had to dodge some hurtled sofa pillows, a paperback book, and an emery board to escape.

Fifteen

Shelley came over a few minutes later. "Anything you need help with?"

"Not a thing," Jane said, still laughing silently over Mel's abrupt departure as she limped back to the living room. She'd learned she could go a few steps without the crutches if she took it carefully and stayed on carpeted floors.

"I saw Mel leave in a hurry. Did he tell you anything new about Julie Jackson?" Shelley asked.

Jane started repeating what he'd said about the attack, but Shelley interrupted. "What about the flowers with the strange note?"

Jane slapped her forehead. "I completely forgot to ask."

"How could you forget, Jane? That seems to me to be a very important part of the case. It was a warning, and by saying 'You're next,' it suggested that an earlier crime had been committed."

"I hadn't really thought about it that way, but you're right," Jane said, easing herself back onto the sofa.

"I only realized it myself about an hour ago. You can't imagine how hard it was to wait for Mel to leave, so I wouldn't be butting in."

"I don't dare call him and ask now," Jane said. "Mel's working three cases and just went home to try to catch some rest. I can't believe I didn't realize the significance of the note before. Why is this foot injury going to my brain?"

"What else did he tell you?" Shelley asked, heading for the kitchen. "Want a soda?"

"No, thanks, but help yourself."

When Shelley was settled in with a Diet Coke and handful of Wheat Thins, Jane reviewed the conversation with Mel. Unlike her guilt at telling Miss Winstead too much, she knew Mel was aware that she'd tell Shelley everything and they'd keep it to themselves. In fact, Shelley would be more reliably silent than Jane herself had been.

"So he does suspect one of the class members?" Shelley asked.

"Not exactly 'suspect.' I had the feeling it was just one more thing he felt he needed to check out to be thorough. Just in case."

"It sounds like he's got a full plate of suspects already," Shelley agreed. "But it *could* have some connection to someone we've met. Ursula is an obvious madwoman, and that Jones guy who looks like he gets his hair cut every three days seems more than a little bit strange. If Miss Winstead is telling the absolute truth about her cousin, Dr. Eastman isn't a very nice man either. Miss Winstead herself is frightening. Such anger."

"But not at Julie. And justified," Jane said. "If, as you say, it's the truth."

"Yes, but she's a strong-minded woman. It wouldn't surprise me completely if she just decided to eradicate someone."

Jane laughed. "So are you firm-minded!"

"That's why she worries me," Shelley said with a smile. "Seriously, I only get irritated with incompetents and fools. I don't hold lifelong grudges against anyone but the IRS. After they had those public hearings, their threats got smarmier, but they're still threats . . ."

"Shelley!" Jane exclaimed, having heard this all before.

"What I'm getting to is that I guess if Miss Winstead were to try to bump someone off, it would have been Dr. Eastman a long time ago. No real reason to wait several decades."

"I wonder if her hints that Stefan Eckert was up to some sort of hanky-panky were true."

"That *was* an odd thing for her to say. Maybe she's just naturally suspicious of everyone. Especially someone who can line up speakers that she couldn't manage to get. I'm sure that irritated her. I think she expects to get her way by ordering people around and hates it when someone like Stefan outwits her with pure charm and good looks. Did you notice how much he looks like George Stephanopoulas?" Shelley said.

"I certainly did, but what I'm most anxious to look at is Miss Winstead's garden," Jane said. "I felt that the other gardens we've visited really said something about the gardeners' personalities."

"Oh, dear! Then I'm in trouble," Shelley said. "Mine isn't even really mine. It's out on loan."

"So will mine be," Jane said smugly. "I followed your bad example and called the nursery. My garden 'arrives' tomorrow afternoon. And I have a water feature!"

"Jane! You didn't! What fools we're making of ourselves. I'm really regretting my pretense. The others are going to see right through us and despise us."

"Why? It's not as if we won't enjoy having nice things for people to see. And we might both want to keep them all instead of letting them go back to the nursery."

Shelley looked embarrassed. "I've been looking around and had already decided I'm going to keep the stuff I rented. The yard looks so nice now."

"What wimps we are," Jane said. "I've already committed to keeping the little fountain. I saw it when Mike showed me around the nursery last week and longed for it."

"Then you should have it," Shelley said authoritatively.

Jane's calf muscle was cramping, and she shifted

around to get more comfortable. "Does it strike you as strange that the only ones of us who found something to like in Ursula's garden were you and I and Miss Winstead?"

"Naturally we liked some of it because we're open-minded," Shelley said. "But yes, I was surprised to see Miss Winstead taking notes."

"Don't you wish you could have seen the notes?"

Shelley looked at Jane and asked, "What are you suggesting?"

"Maybe her notes weren't exactly about the garden. That's all. Maybe they were about Ursula herself."

"Why would you think that? Oh, if she were a suspect . . ."

They both fell silent for a moment, then Shelley said, "You have half an excuse to be speculating wildly, what with the foot, and the crutches, and Kipsy Topper and all. But there's really no reason to think anybody in the class had anything to do with hurting Julie even if Mel insists they're second-string suspects."

"I suppose you're right. But Julie Jackson knew some of them. Dr. Eastman for one. She worked out the schedule with Stefan Eckert. Her own sister joined the class. And Miss Winstead has been in touch with her as well. What if one or even all of the others also knew her? We're all in the same neighborhood and have been for a pretty long time. Even I had met her at a city council meeting and remembered who she was."

"But isn't it more logical that one of the men she was always being seen with is more likely?"

Jane smiled. "Maybe so, but we don't know who they are and can hardly gossip about them. Anyway, this is taking my mind off The Dreaded Kipsy *and* my foot."

Mike was late again. At eleven o'clock as Jane was wondering how to get upstairs with her book, her last cup of decaf coffee, and the clean towels for her bathroom, Katie stormed down the steps. She was livid with sibling rivalry. "Mike's not that much older than me."

"Not much older than I . . ." Jane corrected her.

"Why can't I come and go whenever I want like he does?"

"Because you're younger. And, much as I hate to say it, a girl. Could you help me carry up some of these things?"

"Mom! You're positively medieval! I'm not a dumb little girl. I'm a young woman. If you just got me a can of Mace and a cell phone, I'd be perfectly safe anywhere."

"You forgot to mention the car to get anywhere," Jane said sarcastically.

"No, I didn't. You bought Mike a truck. Why not me?"

"Because you're too young. And you're not as good at driving yet as he was when I got him the truck."

This was the honest truth. Katie wasn't making progress with driving safely. She was too busy looking around at boys walking down the street, checking her

122

lipstick while driving. Forgetting to lock the car. Forgetting to put on the parking brake. Dumping chewing gum in the ashtray. But Jane hated being that honest.

For one thing, Katie was in a snit and jealous of her big brother, and would think it was an excuse for depriving her of her rights.

For another, Jane's own background wasn't anything like Katie's. She hadn't learned to drive until she was almost twenty, because her diplomat family always traveled in limos or trains or taxis or planes. They'd never lived in the same place for much more than six months, and it was never enough to get really familiar with any area, and she simply didn't need to drive until she came home to America for college.

Were daughters always so much more difficult to raise and protect than sons?

And for that matter, was her older son going off the rails after so many years of being so sensible and responsible?

Jane felt seriously tired.

Instead of continuing the argument, Jane had a brainstorm. "Katie, I have an idea. Carry up the coffee cup and towels and I'll tell you about it."

When Jane finally got to her bedroom, Katie was sprawled on her bed, petting the cats and teasing them with a string, but still looking sulky. "So what's the idea?"

"How about you and Jenny taking a cooking class for the rest of the summer? You'd both have fun, and it would be a way for me to pay back Jenny's folks for

123

taking you to France with them. And it would save me some pain and hassle."

Katie was determined to stay mad at her mother, but the idea obviously appealed to her. The rest of the summer vacation must have been looming over her as much as it was Jane. "You'd pay for both of us? And let us practice here?"

That was a scary thought, but Jane said, "Of course. As long as you clean up after yourselves. I'll even give you two a grocery allowance."

Katie was still trying to maintain her sulk, and strolled away saying, "I guess I'll ask Jenny what she thinks."

But once she was out of the bedroom, Jane could hear Katie running down the hall to call Jenny on her extension.

Sixteen

"Cooking lessons!" Shelley exclaimed the next morning as she was helping Jane into the van. "What a good idea. Could we sign Denise up as well? I'd do anything to get her out from underfoot—take them to the lessons and make sure they clean up your kitchen."

"Yes to Denise, yes to driving them, but no to cleaning. You know you'd end up doing it yourself. Part of any job is tidying up as you go along. That's as important in cooking as the ingredients."

"You're right. Are all your parts and paraphernalia in the van now?"

As she took off backwards in the driveway at a speed Jane wouldn't have driven going forward, Shelley said, "I heard Mike's truck come home after midnight."

"I didn't," Jane said. "I woke suddenly at three A.M. and went to see if he was home. I got a crutch stuck in the legs of that foul little table in the upstairs hall, the one that's overbalanced, and woke the whole house up. The kids complained, the cats scattered, and Willard nearly barked himself into a full-fledged fit."

"My aunt Eleanor had a rule you should know about grown kids coming back home. She said the standards in her house were up to her. It didn't matter that they didn't have to come home at a certain time and check in when they were in college or living elsewhere, but when they stayed with her, they were her children and had to live up to her standards."

"And did it work?"

"My cousin Bill got divorced at thirty and moved in with her for a month. He had an eleven-o'clock curfew. If he was so much as a minute late, Aunt Eleanor wouldn't fix him breakfast. Bill *lived* for breakfast."

"I'm going to have to have a talk with Mike. May I cite you as my authority?"

"Cite away."

They were the first to arrive at the classroom. Ursula came moments later, having an intense discussion with Miss Winstead about Chinese computer-geek immi-

125

grants being banned from getting visas. Somehow the House of Windsor seemed to figure in the theory, but it was impossible to guess whether the Chinese immigrants were the Good Guys or the Bad. But clearly Queen Elizabeth was on the baddies' side. Miss Winstead was preoccupied and had obviously tuned Ursula out, merely nodding and making neutral noises.

Ursula abandoned Miss Winstead when she spotted Jane. "I've got a whole new menu for you tonight. You'll love it. You wash, dry, brown, and grind rye seed from the nursery. Grass seed, my dear. Plain old grass seed. Be sure it's pesticide-free, of course, and it makes the most wonderful muffins to spread with butter flavoring added to tofu. Mine's baking dry right now, and this evening I'll grind it and make you bread."

"No," Jane said firmly. "It sounds interesting, but I'm signing my daughter and two of her friends up for a cooking class today and I really must eat whatever they serve. It's a sacrifice, naturally, but what can a mother do?"

"What a good idea. There's a health food store across town that holds cooking classes. I'll give you the phone number." Ursula rummaged in one of her bags, dropping a computer disk, a huge pair of orange-tinted plastic sunglasses, and a tattered facial tissue on the floor, and finally came up with a scrap of paper and a pencil.

"I sometimes give classes there myself," she said, handing the phone number to Jane. As Jane folded the paper to put it in her pocket, she couldn't help but notice that it was on the back of an advertisement for naturally grown cotton made into bras by downtrodden Mexican immigrants.

"Thank you, Ursula," Jane said with a forced smile.

Arnold Waring and Charles Jones must have met up in the parking lot, because they were well into a conversation about a motion that was supposed to be coming before the town council about what color gardening hoses could be left out in front yards. They were in accord that it was nobody's business but the homeowner's and were each goading the other into attending the meeting and speaking to the issue.

Stefan was just behind them and waiting patiently outside the door until Arnie and Charles finally got out of the way. He sat down behind Shelley and Jane and sorted out some files he'd brought along, mumbling to himself and putting sticky notes on some of the papers.

Jane interrupted him to ask if he knew whether Geneva Jackson was coming along today. He replied that she'd caught up to him at the nearest stop sign and waved him over to say she was going to the hospital to visit her sister, now that Julie was well enough to fend off Geneva's hearty good cheer, which drove sick people wild.

Dr. Eastman finally arrived, winded from hurrying and looking a bit frayed at the edges. Jane wondered if something had happened to him since the day before, or whether Miss Winstead's presence was finally unraveling him.

He looked over the class and said, "Miss Jackson's sister, Geneva, found some of Dr. Julie Jackson's notes she'd prepared for this class. She was tidying up the office when the police finished their examination and came across the file. So instead of the material I'd prepared for today, I think we should go over some of the material she had ready for you. And after that we'll take a tour of Miss Winstead's garden and Mr. Jones's. If you remember, they live next door to one another."

He then launched into what would have been Julie Jackson's talk. It was clearly geared for amateurs and was far more interesting to the group than anything Dr. Eastman had said, even though he was reading it with obvious boredom with the basic essentials.

Shelley and Jane took copious notes. The beginning was about soil conditions and was the first time Jane thought she might just eventually understand what grew in acid soil and what preferred alkaline conditions. She'd probably forget it later, but she'd have the clear listings in her notebook. Julie Jackson's voice, coming through Dr. Eastman's vocal cords, was clear and concise. Lists of common plants that liked acid soil in alphabetical order. What to do to alkaline soil to grow them well. Another list of sun and shade plants. Hostas, she said, could take more sun *or* shade than most people thought.

Dr. Jackson was theoretically opposed to strong chemicals, but admitted everyone needed at least one bottle of weed killer and described how, when, and where to use it, and not use it, and how to protect yourself, the good plants, and the pets and children from the poison.

Furthermore, she listed plants you didn't want to have in a garden if children or pets might try to eat them. The first on the list was monkshood. The second was oleander.

Jane was scribbling like mad and so was Shelley. They'd compare their notes later and fill in the blanks. Jane made a note to tell Shelley about the mystery she'd read once in which someone at a hot-dog cookout was given an oleander stick instead of a harmless one to skewer a hot dog. What was the name of the author?

Dr. Eastman had read Julie's speech so quickly that the class ended early on a somewhat breathless note. A couple of people wanted to backtrack and ask questions. "How do you have your soil tested?" Ursula asked.

Dr. Eastman explained that specialty nurseries might have testing kits, or one could contact the Agricultural Department to provide the material to do the testing.

Mention of a federal agency didn't go down well with Ursula. "How would I know if they were telling me the truth?" she said. "Everybody in the government lies."

Dr. Eastman, who hadn't been subjected to as much of her philosophy as Jane had, merely looked at her with curiosity. "Why would anyone deceive you about soil acidity?"

Ursula waved this comment away with a gesture that

dislodged a small disposable camera from somewhere on her person.

Stefan Eckert asked, "Do Dr. Jackson's notes say anything about water gardens? And the kind of plants that are best for this area?"

"I don't believe so," Dr. Eastman said. "But there's a lot of information available from the county extension office. Shall we adjourn the class and go see Miss Winstead's and Mr. Jones's gardens early?"

Charles Jones was on his feet at once. "Excellent idea."

Jane murmured to Shelley that this was a good plan. It would allow them to get home early so she could arrange for the cooking lessons and be home when her "rented" garden arrived.

They rushed along to Charles Jones's house, which was as tidy and boring as he was. A front lawn as neat and well clipped as Dr. Eastman's surrounded a small, absolutely symmetrical, colonial-style home. The evergreen shrubs flanking the front door were clipped into absolutely perfect box shapes. The sidewalks and driveway hadn't so much as one errant leaf or blade of grass ruining their pristine condition.

"I hope my tires are clean enough to park here," Shelley said, pulling the van up the driveway.

Miss Winstead wasn't with them this time because her house was the second on the tour and she'd driven herself to class. She parked her car in her own driveway and strolled along the sidewalk to greet them. "Don't even think about walking on the grass," she advised. "The front yard is wired up somehow to turn on blinding lights to keep kids and dogs from daring to step off the walkways."

Charles himself arrived a moment later, and parked a boxy new Volkswagen on the street so his guests could use the driveway. "I'm so eager to show you everything," he said as Jane was levering herself out of the front passenger seat of Shelley's van.

"Should we go around this side of the house?" Shelley asked.

"No. There are no gates. We have to go through the house," he replied, waving them toward the front door. He opened a series of complicated locks and hurried ahead, presumably to turn off various alarm systems. Then he stood in the open door welcoming the others, who had all arrived at the same time.

Jane and Shelley looked around the living room. It was large but sparsely furnished, with neutral colors and bookshelves filled with computer manuals, and no ornaments whatsoever. The boxy furniture was stark and vaguely Scandinavian, and lined up like it was still on display in a furniture store.

Charles escorted them through a hall and into a kitchen that was as spotless as he was and out the back door into the yard.

There was very little grass back here. But many gardens. As sparse as the house itself. Vast areas of mulch highlighted individual specimen plants. The whole area was laid out like a grid, with square gray blocks as pathways, and each single plant was carefully labeled.

It was *so* Charles Jones.

Jane worked her way along a path and leaned forward to examine an interesting-looking perfectly round plant with deep red blooms and almost black centers with yellow stamens. MONARCH'S VELVET CINQUEFOIL, the label said, followed by the unpronounceable Latin nomenclature. It was the single plant in the bed. There wasn't even a nice ground cover around it, just boring mulch. And the next bed was a small grouping of DELPHINIUM ASTOLAT, so the label read. Six tall spikes of ruffled pink flowers, all carefully staked. Again, isolated in their splendor and looking beautiful, but lonely.

"Why is this so depressing?" Shelley said quietly and sounding genuinely sad.

"Because it's so terribly regimented," Jane said. "The flowers are absolutely perfect and beautiful, but stand like soldiers in separate companies lined up for a picture. And look at the solid fence all around the yard. It's like a prison for the poor flowers, each in its own little naked cell."

Ursula, across the yard, was looking downright mournfully at a plum tree that had been torturously trained to complete perfection. Miss Winstead was examining an enormous Bressingham Blue hosta with leaves that overlapped like a drawing of the ideal hosta. Her thin arms were crossed as if she were in some sort of pain. Arnold Waring was bending over to read a tag in an area where the plant was gone. Apparently executed and removed because it hadn't lived up to Jones's standard. "It was a peony," Arnie said to no one in particular.

"Probably one of those big gorgeous ones that flop around no matter what you try to do," Shelley replied.

Even Dr. Eastman, whose own garden was rigidly controlled to some extent, looked alarmed and disappointed.

Only Charles Jones was smiling. "Aren't they lovely?" he said to Stefan Eckert of a stand of hollyhocks in a vibrant red. Eckert merely nodded and moved on to the next little prison cell of flowers. A large yellow rosebush was held in place by a green metal cage and had given up fighting its confinement.

"I can't stand this," Jane said, heading back to the house to escape.

"We must find a way to thank the poor man for showing it to us," Shelley said, holding out an arm to steady Jane as she lurched along.

"I guess we must. He obviously loves what he's done," Jane said with sorrow. "Isn't that unbelievable?"

Seventeen

Jane was so depressed by Charles Jones's garden that all she wanted to do was go home and eat a whole lot of fudge and try to take a very long nap. She begged Shelley to run away with her, but Shelley said, "You'd be sorry if you missed Miss Winstead's garden."

"You mean she'd make sure I was sorry?"

Shelley laughed. "No, although she might. She and Charles both admitted that their gardens couldn't be more different." She kept her voice low as Miss Winstead was standing only a few feet away and urging everyone along next door.

Jane struggled a bit going up the sidewalk to Miss Winstead's home. There was quite a rise to the south. Instead of going around the house, they were invited to come through the front. Her house wasn't exactly what Jane had expected of the tough librarian. It was feminine but strong. Floral wallpaper, but in bold colors. A lot of good furniture, two small leather sofas, a modernistic dining room table and chairs with bargello needlepoint seats in mauve and federal blue. A pair of chairs that looked as if they might have been Frank Lloyd Wright or a good imitation. There were a lot of pictures on the walls, some very old-fashioned with classical themes, a few more modern ones that were Picasso-ish. A mix that, surprisingly, worked perfectly together.

Passing through a huge kitchen that was equipped for a chef, they entered the backyard.

And Jane, who was still recovering from such a large, professional kitchen, gasped.

It was a quintessential English cottage garden. There were lots of old brick paths with lush moss, stone terraces, well-clipped hedges. There was very little lawn, but a vast profusion of flowers. Tall, perfect cream hollyhocks formed a backup to a riot of bachelor buttons in a mix of colors that in turn were framed in front by a delicious group of huge chartreuse hostas, which were kept from overrunning the slate path by a formal box hedge, no more than six inches high and perfectly clipped.

No area was quite on a level with any other area. The yard sloped down to the right, and was terraced expertly with fieldstone in one spot, with a waterfall of lobelia in front of a stand of coral gladiolas and maiden grass. Another terrace was of dark granite blocks with pink verbena cascading over the front, and behind it a hedge of wild white roses climbing rough wood trellises that looked as if they had to be at least a hundred years old.

"You're surprised?" Miss Winstead asked.

"Surprised? Stunned to the core," Jane said. "This could be in Kent, England, instead of Chicago."

"There are secret gardens," Miss Winstead said smugly. "See if you can find them."

Jane nearly forgot about her foot. There were paths leading through these gardens to "rooms" not seen from the house. She laboriously worked at climbing some shallow stone steps to the hollyhock garden, which led unexpectedly into a formal sitting area with a verdigris table and four chairs underneath a loggia covered with wisteria with a trunk the size of a large man's thigh.

Almost invisible behind the gladiolas was another "room" that had a spectacular vine with red trumpet flowers covering it.

"That's my only really big mistake," Miss Winstead said, having followed Jane.

"How can it be a mistake? It's beautiful! So lush and such a brilliant color."

"But it's a thug," Miss Winstead said. "It spreads like wild, sort of like kudzu but prettier. I know people who have had it near their house and it's put down roots that go under the house, and plants come in cracks in the basement. Cracks it apparently causes. It tears down fences, forcing itself between the slats and moving into other yards. This fall I'm taking it out if I can. I didn't know enough about it before I planted it. It was a spur-of-the-moment purchase because I liked the flowers and the shape. It will probably take years of weed killer to totally eradicate it."

"That's a pity."

"Yes, it is. But I can't let a vandal take over the yard. Come see the pool."

"There's a pool?"

It was in the lowest spot and was fed by a stream falling over lovely round river rocks. A fountain that looked like a well-greened copper Neptune spouted water from his trident, and goldfish frolicked color-fully around the water lilies below. Black ones, orange ones, and a pair of huge gold ones that looked like they were truly armored in gold plate. "That pair are koi," Miss Winstead said. "I'm afraid I'm eventually going to have to find another home for them when they get so big that they eat everyone else. They can get absolutely huge."

A frog was startled by their approach and leaped into the pool like kids do cannonballs into a swimming pool. Most of the water lilies were lemon-sherbet yellow, and another plant had sprays of lacy flower heads dropping over the edge. "What are those?" Jane asked.

"Oh, just common papyrus," Miss Winstead said.

"I've never seen papyrus growing for real," Jane said. "It doesn't look common at all. Isn't this a huge amount of work? The water is crystal-clear. No green goo at all."

"I just clean the filters about every five days. It's a messy job, but with natural biological deterrents added, enzymes that starve algae, it keeps clean. And I have a pair of men who winterize it for me. It was they who put the pool in to start with and they know it well."

"Winterize?"

"They net it in the fall to keep the oak leaves from the yard behind me from falling into the water—they would make the water acid and eventually rot and cause pollution. My men come back out when the leaves have all fallen and take the leaves and net away. Then they catch the fish and snails and frogs and put them in big buckets of water, drain and clean the pool, turn off the fountain, refill the pool with fresh dechlorinated water, and put a bubbler in to keep an area clear to get rid of the methane that would be trapped and kill the fish and plants. They're the same young men who constructed the terraces and paths over the years as I found materials I liked."

"You go shopping for rocks? Where?"

Miss Winstead looked at Jane somewhat pityingly and said, "At rock suppliers. The ones at most nurseries that even carry rocks have such artificial-looking junk."

"You're so fortunate to have help with this," Jane said. "But I bet you do all the gardening yourself."

Miss Winstead looked surprised. "Of course I do. It's all to my taste and who would know my taste except myself?"

"How do you keep that moss alive in the bricks? I've always wanted a little moss garden in a bowl, and I kill moss faster than anyone can believe."

"Never water, only mist," Miss Winstead said. "And make sure it's in a cool place with shade."

"I'm glad to know you can get around well when you want to," Shelley said, joining them at the side of the pool. "I'm going to remember this when you try to convince me you're helpless. Miss Winstead, this is the most beautiful garden I've ever seen."

Miss Winstead allowed herself a moment of preening, then said, "A person who really wants something badly enough will do anything to have it. It's a lot of work, but all enjoyable. If I lived in the South where I had to keep up with weeds and insects all year round, I'd have an apartment instead of gardening. And the only plants would be violets on the windowsills."

"Why is that?" Shelley asked.

"Because I love putting the garden to bed in the late fall. Tearing out things that didn't work out, planting bulbs, and mulching the delicate things. Then I have all winter to plan the next spring and summer without any work at all. Just waiting for plant catalogs to drool over."

The rest of the group was gathering at the side of the pool. Miss Winstead disappeared for a moment and came back with tiny packets of fish food, which the goldfish and koi greedily gobbled up, mouths agape as if they were starving. Arnold Waring smiled at their antics and so did Charles Jones, who quickly ruined the smile by saying, "Didn't I say Miss Winstead's garden and mine were very different?"

He sounded so proud of this, as if he had no sense of how much the rest of the class loved Miss Winstead's garden. Or any concept of how dreary his own was.

Stefan Eckert looked as if he were dreaming, his eyes half-closed with contentment. Even Ursula was impressed. "This is what I'd like my yard to look like," she said, quietly for once.

Dr. Eastman said, "Fine work, Miss Winstead. How long has this garden been here?"

"Only five years come fall," she replied. "Not counting the two years I spent figuring out where I wanted the walls and walks and hedges."

"That's the true measure of a real gardener," Dr. Eastman said. "The patience to wait, the planning ahead . . ."

"And the pure mean-spiritedness to rip up anything

139

or anyone that doesn't work out," Miss Winstead said.

Dr. Eastman paled, but didn't respond.

Eighteen

"Boy, that was scary," Jane said as she hoisted herself into Shelley's van.

"Aren't you glad her remarks weren't aimed at us?" Shelley said, making a little shiver. "If I'd been Dr. Eastman, I'd be installing a new security system right now. We better hurry home. I've got to take the girls to their cooking lesson. They're starting a couple days late, but they can catch up in the next round of classes. The teacher says she covers the same thing the first day of each session, but after that it's different recipes."

"Does this mean they can take lessons the whole rest of the summer!" Jane exclaimed. "And by the way, what did this first group of lessons cost? I need to reimburse you."

"Only five bucks a day," Shelley said. "But we had to pay for the days they missed."

After she'd pocketed Jane's check, Shelley abandoned her and gathered up their daughters and drove off to fetch the third girl, Katie's best friend, Jenny. Jane was glad she had a good excuse not to drive a summer car pool. As soon as Todd was old enough to drive, she'd be through with car pools, except for blind kids she drove to their special school once a week.

She'd once filled in for one of the other women who'd broken her arm two years earlier and was getting time off in kind until she could drive again.

Enough of thinking about the distant future. The immediate future loomed.

She was going to have to do some work before the nursery guys delivered her "instant" garden. She went out the back door to find the pooper-scooper in the garage. She left it by the patio table and spent a full fifteen minutes nudging along the trash bin onto the patio. She'd always figured poop scooping was somehow inherently a male job. She'd always made Mike or Todd do it. But today neither of them was around. And even Katie was gone. Not that Katie would acknowledge such a request.

In her travels around the yard, she got the tip of the crutch stuck in a chipmunk hole, and put it down once on a fallen branch that rolled away under her. But she managed to stay upright while she quartered the grass. Max and Meow, fresh from hunting mice in the field behind her house, abandoned their favorite activity to hang around with her.

"You guys are good cats. You do your business somewhere else."

Max tried to rub against her leg in appreciation, but she moved the crutch accidentally and he fled for his life.

She'd barely wrestled the trash bin back in the garage when a big truck pulled up in front of the house. The first guy out of the truck lowered a plank and dollied off a huge box. "Where do you want this thing, lady?"

"Is it my fountain? In the middle of the yard, I thought."

"It takes electricity. Have you got a really long cord?" he said.

She wondered if this was sarcasm or a really stupid idea that sounded all right to him.

"Oh . . . no, I don't. I guess it'll have to go on the patio. I think there's an outlet by the back door. I never thought about what makes a fountain work."

The next guy off the truck was her son Mike. He was grinning. "Show-off," he said as he passed her with a pot of purple and white impatiens. "Where does this go?"

Jane, as always, had made a list of what she'd ordered. She was an inveterate list maker. The kind of list maker who, when doing something not on the list, adds it so it can be crossed out. But her map of the yard was pretty awful. It had come out like a trapezoid instead of a rectangle.

"The big pot goes at the left end of the patio. The little one goes on the table. You do have the new umbrella for the table with you, right?"

She gave Mike the map and went to watch the man installing the fountain. It came in a lot of pieces that didn't look as if they'd all fit together. There was a pump (at least she assumed that was what it was) and tubing, clamps, and screws. The guy who was putting it together didn't even look at the directions. He must have done a lot of these before. He had a level and set the bottom basin in place, nudging small flat rocks under it until he was satisfied it was sitting properly. That was something she'd have never thought of.

This was the sort of thing, like scooping poop, that men were designed for. But she was glad once again that she had the cast and crutches as a good excuse for not being useful. Being a temporary invalid had a few benefits.

Apparently the man assembling the fountain hadn't noticed, however, and said, "Bring me a hose. We'll fill her up and see how she works." *Why do men always consider appliances feminine?* Jane wondered. The repairman she'd had in to fix the dishwasher two weeks ago did the same thing.

Jane stumbled to the reel where the hose was wound up, got drips on her sleeves while disconnecting the sprinkler, and dragged the hose to the patio, water dribbling down the side of her shorts and into her cast.

But it was worth the effort. Once the fountain starting circulating, it was delightful. The outlet at the top was concealed, and a slow, clear stream of water burbled out from it, trickling down into the first basin, filling it up and cascading into the second. Such a pleasant thing to hear water running so sweetly.

While she'd been watching the fountain installer and hauling around the hose, Mike and another young man had set out planters crammed with flowers where she'd indicated on the crummy map. She turned away from the fountain and was astonished at how nice the patio looked. So colorful and crowded with flowers in lovely pots. She had the awful feeling that she'd convince herself that she had to keep it all instead of renting it. It made the patio so inviting. She found herself looking at the table and thinking hard about getting some drinking glasses and little luncheon plates that would pick up the color of the flowers.

Show-off, she said to herself.

The workers were almost ready to leave in half an hour. When one of the other summer helpers who was aimlessly sweeping fallen petals off the patio asked how she had hurt herself, she told him she'd fallen off a runway while doing a fashion show. Mike overheard this and gouged her shoulder, laughing. He'd raided the box of doughnuts that Shelley had brought earlier and shared them with the other guys.

"Mom, this really does look nice. I'm glad you did this," Mike told her. "Are you going to spring for keeping the planters?"

Jane nodded and said, "I'm afraid so. It's going to cost the earth, but it looks so nice. You'll mow the lawn tomorrow evening, won't you? I'd hate to lose someone out there."

When the doughnuts were gone, and plants watered, the fountain guy gave Jane a wad of printed instructions about maintaining the fountain.

"Could I maybe put a few really tiny fishes in it?" she asked, thinking how the flash of goldfish would improve the looks of the fountain.

The man looked at her as if she'd lost her mind.

"Fishes get it dirty, have to be fed, and what would you do with them in the winter?"

He had a good point.

"Mom, try not to get carried away," Mike warned. "Remember what happened to you when you tried to cartwheel down the runway at that fashion show."

The crew departed, strengthened by Jane's doughnuts. Only then did the cats reemerge from hiding in the field. They were roaming around cautiously, sniffing everything new to determine if these pots of stuff were friends or enemies. Jane levered herself down onto one of the patio chairs, leaned back, and looked around with an enormous smile. This wouldn't fool the real gardeners in the class, but it was so pretty she didn't care.

As she sipped at her soft drink she'd laboriously brought outside in her waistband, she thought about the tour that morning. Miss Winstead's garden was magnificent. It would be pure joy to have a garden like that. But an enormous amount of work, because Jane couldn't imagine having or spending the money for rocks and workers.

Her mind drifted naturally to the end of the visit, when Miss Winstead had made that remark about being able to tear out anything or anyone who didn't satisfy a gardener. Meaning Dr. Eastman and his late wife. And she thought about Shelley's remarks about getting a security system. Jane didn't really believe Miss Winstead was a physical threat to Dr. Eastman, but she was a substantial psychological threat. She tried to imagine what horror it would be to have someone hate you so much that she went around to all your speeches just to make a fool of you and make nasty personal remarks. Especially around other people.

She put both feet up on another chair, carefully balanced the crutches on a third, and closed her eyes halfway—trying to picture her garden looking like Miss Winstead's.

Jane was sound asleep in the patio chair, a bad crick in her neck, when Shelley dropped the girls off. She was embarrassed by being caught sleeping, much less slumped inelegantly in a patio chair.

"Mom!" Katie said. "We learned to make chicken cordon bleu! We're fixing it tonight for you. Mrs. Nowack stopped at the grocery store and let us buy the stuff. You owe her twenty-three dollars and six cents."

The girls went in the house, giggling with the shrillness that only teenaged females could stand to hear. Shelley strolled into Jane's yard. "Sleeping? You really are turning into a sloth."

"How did you know I was sleeping?"

"You have a print of the top edge of the chair on the back of your neck. It's a nice waffle look."

"Okay, okay. So I took a little nap. How do you like the yard?"

"It's gorgeous. You even got a shrubbery over by the fence. What is it?"

"A burning bush. Mike threw it in with the rest

146

because he said I'm going to like it. It looks pretty boring to me."

"It'll be fantastic—if a bit small—in the fall," Shelley said. "It's one of those things Suzie Williams has in her side yard."

"Oh, those are great bushes. I had no idea what they were called. I understand I owe you more money."

"No, the shopping today was almost the same cost as that pork roast you picked up for me last week that I've never reimbursed you for."

"Do you really think the girls can make chicken cordon bleu?"

"Only if I supervise. Which I intend to do. Denise tried to make scrambled eggs a while ago and managed to use five bowls, three forks, and about sixteen whisks. And left them all out on the counter to congeal. Three inexperienced girls could destroy your entire kitchen."

Jane struggled to her feet and, in getting the crutches, nearly knocked the flowerpot off the patio table. "I'm not getting much better at this," she said.

"You will," Shelley said as she went in Jane's back door, leaving Jane to make it inside by herself and carry her own empty soda can as well.

Shelley's voice from the kitchen drifted over her. "Denise! Don't just abandon that bowl. Rinse it and use it again!"

Nineteen

The chicken dinner was only a moderate success, at least in Jane and Shelley's view. The girls had opened the oven so often to check on the progress that the chicken itself was ever so slightly underdone when they cut into it.

"Poultry needs to be fully cooked," Jane warned them. "At least pop it in the microwave for a minute to finish it up."

"Microwave?" Katie exclaimed as if her mother had said a dirty word. "The French don't use microwaves. It makes meat like leather."

Jane replied, "The French were among the first countries to develop fabulous dinners with microwaves. I thought everyone knew that."

Jane had made up this statement on the spur of the moment, but she felt she'd delivered it with great style and conviction.

"You lived in France, didn't you?" Shelley's daughter, Denise, asked.

"Off and on for several years," Jane said. One vote for her.

"That isn't what our teacher said," Katie countered. One vote against.

"Ask your teacher if she's ever eaten in France," Shelley suggested.

"I don't mean to discourage you girls, but birds really need to be well done. Put them back in the oven for a little bit if Katie feels so strongly," Jane advised.

"But the broccoli will be cold and soggy if we wait."

"I love cold soggy broccoli!" Shelley said.

"Me, too," Jane added.

The girls did as they were told and the dinner turned out well enough even if the chicken got a bit *too* well done. They had to gnaw it rather than simply eating it. But the taste was good. And they could honestly praise the girls for this without alluding to the texture.

Jane sat back from the table, making her crutches, propped behind her chair, crash to the floor. "Sorry," she said, gathering them up. "Now it's time to clean up."

"We'll put everything in the dishwasher," Katie said. "Then we're going to a movie."

Jane shook her head. "Not until the dishes are done and put away. That's part of cooking."

Shelley took her aside and whispered, "If we want them to learn to cook, we need to give them a little leeway on the icky parts of the process. At least at first."

Jane laughed. "Who was making them wash and reuse the bowls? Not me."

"But . . ." Shelley stopped herself and grinned. Then said to the girls, "You could hand-wash and dry them faster and still get to the movie in time."

Jane had to get outside where she couldn't hear them bashing her plates around in the sink. Shelley brought them both cups of coffee and sat down opposite Jane at the patio table. "Have they broken anything yet?" Jane asked.

"Only a salt shaker," Shelley replied.

"Why were they washing a salt shaker?"

"They weren't. It just got in the way."

Jane sighed. "This seemed such a good idea. Now I'm wondering if we're all going to get ptomaine poisoning."

"Maybe they'll move on to desserts tomorrow," Shelley suggested. "Desserts can't poison anyone."

"The cream can go bad."

"Why are you being so bleak?"

"It's *my* kitchen. You'd be bleak if they were trashing yours. Did you ask them to wash up whatever sticky stuff they got on the floor?"

"I put a mop out for them," Shelley said a little more cheerfully than normal for her. "It's so nice out here with all these plants. Jane, we really ought to learn to garden for ourselves. Picture a sweep of obedient plants in white and pink against your fence. That would be so pretty," she added, trying to cheer Jane up.

"What are obedient plants?"

"Nice little bushy things with spires of flowers. One of the few things that blooms well in the fall. My mother has grown them for years. I'm sure she'd be glad to dig some up for you. They spread so well she has to give baskets of them away every fall or they'd take over her whole yard."

"That doesn't sound very 'obedient' to me."

"The obedient part of the name is supposed to be that

150

you can make them bend every which way you want. They look good with cosmos, which start blooming sooner, but last to frost."

"Whose gardens are we seeing tomorrow?" Jane changed the subject. Right now the idea of digging up part of the yard to put in a real garden was too daunting to consider. Though maybe later, when she wasn't stuck in the cast, it would sound better.

"Arnold Waring's and Stefan Eckert's. Although Stefan doesn't even claim to have a garden. He just wants one. We should have told him that you can rent one. Maybe we should team up with him and collect ideas from plant catalogs."

"Poor old Arnold, trying to keep up his wife's garden. What a chore it must be for him."

"I think he might like it," Shelley said. "It's probably a way he keeps his wife's memory alive and growing."

"Somebody told me once that gardens should die with the gardener," Jane said. "I guess I don't like that view any more than Arnold does. It's sort of like tearing a house down just because the person who built and lived in it is gone."

"You're having such grim thoughts this evening. What's really wrong?" Shelley asked.

Jane shrugged. "I'm meeching. I'm just sick of everything I do being so much more difficult. I've lost my freedom to drive myself. I can't take a shower without trussing up my whole leg. And every time I turn over at night, I bang the cast on my other leg. I had no idea a cast could make such an impact on my daily life. And be so itchy. And just think of how hairy my leg is going to be when it's taken off."

"You'll just wear a long skirt that day, and fling it down to your ankle the moment the cast is gone. It won't be on for long," Shelley said. "It wasn't all that bad a break. I'll bet you get out of it in three or four weeks. And I'm willing to drive you wherever you need to go."

Jane laughed at that. "That's one of the worst parts of the experience!"

"I'm not a bad driver. I've never had an accident that was my fault," Shelley said defensively.

"You're a terrifying driver. You know that. You take pride in taking over any road you're on. Give you an ignition key and you turn into Attila the Hun, conquering the highways of the Western world."

"What a sissy you are," Shelley said. "No sense of adventure at all."

The back door opened. Mel said, "The girls said you two were hiding out here. Jane! What happened to your yard?"

"I broke down and followed Shelley's example and rented a semigarden."

"It looks great." He took the chair between them and patted Jane's arm. "You look glum."

"Thanks. I'm having a pity party about my foot."

"Too bad you didn't break it when you were a kid. Having a cast then is a mark of honor."

Jane made a conscious decision to at least act happy. Nobody was taking her complaints seriously.

"Shelley's trying to get me to plant a real garden when I'm out of the cast."

"Good idea. I could help."

Jane turned and looked at him. "How? Why?"

"I'd love to have a weekend or two renting guy machines. High loaders, trenchers, stuff like that."

"It must really be a guy thing. I don't even know what those things are for," Jane said with a smile. "And they sound like something that would scare the cats out of their skins. How's Julie Jackson doing today?"

Mel said, "She's getting better physically. Still no memory of anything about the attack. Apparently the hospital is willing to send her home in a day or two, so long as her sister and brother-in-law can stay over to watch her closely for a few days."

"I'm glad she's getting better," Jane said, "but I really meant, how is the case going?"

"I was too busy with another case nearly all day. I made a couple of stabs at getting in touch with Dr. Eastman. He doesn't seem to ever be home. I'm afraid I might have upset the boy who answers the phone by calling three or four times. Now he's worried about where his boss has gone."

"Aren't you?" Shelley asked.

"Not really. Why should I be?"

"Because the woman who was supposed to teach the class was seriously injured, and what if it had something to do with the class itself?"

"But, Jane, why would anyone try to stop her

teaching what she writes about all the time?"

Jane hated it when Mel was so reasonable and she hadn't a good answer.

"I'll catch him later tonight," Mel said. "He might have just driven up for the day to the place he has up north. That's what the boy thought." He looked toward the house. "Were there any leftovers from your dinner? I didn't even get lunch today."

"One piece of leather chicken," Jane said.

"I think I'll stop for fast food," Mel said, getting up. He kissed Jane in a preoccupied manner and said, "Perk up, honey."

When he'd gone, Shelley and Jane looked at each other for a long moment.

"Are you thinking what I am?" Shelley asked.

"Yes. What's become of Dr. Eastman?"

Twenty

Jane was giving the cats fresh cat food about eight o'clock that night when the doorbell rang. It was Arnie Waring again. This time with a crock-pot recipe of Darlene's three-beans, onion, and ham recipe in a heavy plastic container with a towel around it.

"I'm sorry I'm dropping by so late," he said, "but I started this after the garden tours and had to wait until it was done. I guess you've had your dinner already, but it heats up real good the next day." He set the container down and unwrapped it; it even contained homemade crackers in a well-sealed plastic bag.

Jane was touched. "Arnie, you're just trying to fatten me up. I don't need fattening. This is so sweet of you, though. And it smells fantastic."

"You could use some weight. I was always glad that Darlene was a bit plump. It made her even prettier."

"I guess that's true of some women," Jane said.

Arnie went on, "This was my wife's favorite recipe, and mine, too. She made it every Wednesday night, which this is. I always cook it up on Wednesdays."

Jane was torn. She wanted to say, *Darlene is gone. Get your own life.*

But that would only hurt his feelings. He was devoted to her memory, and duplicating their life before she died probably kept him alive and busy and made his days happier. Maybe this was the only life that could ever be his own.

"How long ago did your wife die?" she asked, hoping it wasn't a tactless question.

"Four years and three weeks ago. I wish you could have known her. She was the best woman in the world. Little, but strong. And so smart. She read all the time. And her gardens were beautiful. I've tried so hard to keep them just as she left them, but I'm not a good gardener. It's sad to see her plants looking so bad."

"I'm sure when we visit your yard tomorrow, somebody will make good suggestions. It won't be me, though. I'm not really a gardener, I'd just like to turn into one," Jane said.

"I don't want to be one," Arnie admitted. "I just owe it to Darlene."

Jane thought for a moment. "Are you sure you owe her that?"

He frowned. "I'm sure."

"I'm sorry if I offended you," Jane said. "It's just that I'm a widow. My husband died in a car wreck, but I've gone on with my own life. So I guess I see it differently."

Jane didn't think she needed to give the whole truth, that Steve had died on an icy bridge while leaving her for another woman.

"But you're young," Arnie said. "I married Darlene when we were both seventeen and we lived together with joy for decades. These things are easier when you're young."

"I guess you're right. I didn't mean to pry or criticize. You're a good man. And I thank you for the beans. They'll be my lunch tomorrow and I'll be thinking of you and Darlene."

Once again Arnie was about to get teary, so he very nearly ran out of the house without even saying goodbye.

Jane felt a bit teary, too. But she'd lied about waiting until tomorrow's lunch. She was already hungry after the mediocre meal the girls had cooked. She scooped out a ladle full of the beans and ham and warmed them up in the microwave. Katie must have smelled the aroma wafting up the stairs, and came down from her room to eat again as well.

"Mom, this is great stuff. Did you make it?"

"No, an old man I know made it with his late wife's recipe."

Katie nibbled a few of the crackers. "These are terrific, too." She finished munching and said, "Our dinner wasn't really very good, was it?"

Jane shook her head sadly. "No, I'm afraid it wasn't. But cooking is an art. It takes practice and experimentation. Sometimes for years. I had no idea how to cook anything at all when I married your father. I'd eaten what the staff of various embassies had cooked through my whole childhood. Then I ate in a dorm in college. And when I finished, I had a roommate who was a good cook and wouldn't let me near the kitchen. Your father nearly starved to death the first whole year we were married, I was so bad at cooking."

"I'd like to be good—at something," Katie said.

"You're already good at a lot of things, Katie. Your grades at school have steadily gotten better and better and I'm so proud of you for that."

"But you say I'm no good at driving."

"Because you aren't yet. You will be when you learn how important it is to keep your eyes and brain on the road instead of what you see around you. You might turn out to be a race driver. Though I pray not!" Jane added with a smile.

"So when do people get to know what they really want to be good at?"

Hard question for a mom who wanted to give good advice.

"Everybody knows when it comes along," Jane said. "I'm still working on being a writer, you know. I've spent a couple years on one book because it's not good enough yet. But like you with driving, the more I do it, the better I get when I focus on the right things. And I'm a pretty good cook when I feel like it, even though I started out badly. And I'm a better driver than Mrs. Nowack."

Katie laughed. "*Everybody's* a better driver than Mrs. Nowack."

Katie rinsed out her bowl, put it in the dishwasher, brushed the cracker crumbs into her hand, and washed them down the disposal before leaving the room.

That's progress, Jane thought.

Jane went to bed early. Mike was still out at ten, and she was fretting that he was getting seriously interested in the bizarre Kipsy Topper. How could he be? She was such a deliberately unattractive girl. And appeared to have no personality at all. Or, if the conversation she overheard when Shelley was grilling her was any indication, an unformed and insecure personality.

She crawled into bed, knocking her left shin against the cast. She'd had it on more than half a week now. In light of her talk with Katie, it was time to quit whining about it and learn to get around better. No more scooting up and down the stairs on her bottom, no more letting people help her in and out of vehicles.

After all, this was nothing. A broken bone in a foot was trivial. It wasn't on a scale with breast cancer or some other dangerous disease. She'd been a wimp and should have been thinking it was a good thing she had nothing worse wrong with her body and health.

When she comfortably settled into bed, she realized she'd brought the wrong book upstairs. It was *The Arms of Krupp*, not the mystery she intended to read tonight. She crawled back out of bed, picked up the crutches she'd dragged upstairs, and with determination, got to the bottom of the stairs keeping upright. A small victory, but she was learning how to cope and was proud of herself. Starting now, she was no longer an invalid. She was a perfectly able-bodied woman who just happened to have a cast on her leg.

She got back up to her bedroom with only one scary moment at the top step, and started reading the mystery book she'd fetched from the living room. But ten pages into it, she realized she'd read it before and hadn't believed the ending. So what now?

She hoped to be awake when Mike came in. Should she tidy up the closet? It didn't really need tidying. She could strip the bed and wash the sheets, but that would take too long. She suddenly realized how terrific it would be to have something to watch on television. But she'd always resisted having a television in her bedroom for no good reason.

But now she was Woman, competent with crutches, and she deserved one. She'd order it tomorrow. That way she could listen to a program while she was taking a bath, or cleaning upstairs, or simply vegging out early.

Somehow this seemed to her to be a very grown-up decision. Inside, there was still a little of Katie in her. That remnant of insecurity that probably haunts every adult.

Except maybe Shelley.

Twenty-one

When Shelley came out of her house to fetch Jane, she found her friend walking almost normally up and down the driveway.

"Good Lord, I think you've got it!" Shelley exclaimed, clapping her hands.

"I've been experimenting since six this morning," Jane said. "I finally caught on that I do better with one crutch. It substitutes for the bad foot, but I don't need the other one for the good foot. And I don't hang by my armpits with only one. Aren't I great? Watch this!"

She did a slightly awkward half pirouette. "Not bad, huh?" Jane said, grinning.

"What happened to you? Yesterday you were a sad sack, today you're Margot Fonteyn at her peak."

"Two conversations last night," Jane said, opening the door of Shelley's van and expertly hoisting herself up, with her left hand grasping the inside top of the door and hauling the rest of herself and the crutch into the front seat. "One with poor old Arnie—wait till you taste his wife's ham and three-bean stew—and one talk with Katie. Completely different topics, but it cured me of my hypochondria. Could you drive me to buy a television for my bedroom this afternoon?"

Shelley goggled. "I thought I'd never hear you say that. You must be the last person in the neighborhood to succumb. I thought you felt it was immoral or something to have a TV in the bedroom."

"I guess I did. It was stupid and I want one. I suddenly have the overwhelming urge to watch the morning news in bed."

"The pharmacies must be doing well," Shelley said.

"Amazingly well," Jane admitted.

When she'd married into a family-owned pharmacy, they'd had money problems and she'd contributed a smallish inheritance of her own to help them over the slump. Out of gratitude, a document had been drawn up saying if her husband died first, she'd still receive his one-third share of the profits. She'd hoarded the money for the kids' college funds in stocks that were also doing well.

"I see they're putting up another facility in that new mall," Shelley added.

"And they've gone on-line and are raking in Internet sales at a fabulous rate," Jane replied. "I'll never get really rich, but I finally have enough stashed away for college fees and can do a few things for myself. Being stingy is a hard habit to break, but the television for myself is a start."

"Is getting rid of that awful station wagon and filling the chasm in your driveway next?"

"The station wagon still has a few miles to go, but I

really should get a new driveway," Jane said, her eyes lighting up at the thought of getting rid of the World's Worst Pothole.

Shelley shot out of the driveway, talking and looking at Jane. "So Arnie brought you some more food. I think maybe he's getting a crush on you."

"He'll get over it today, if he does. Now that I'm clearly mobile. He was just feeding me because I was acting so helpless. Don't you ever look at what's behind you?"

"I don't care what's behind me," Shelley said with a laugh. "You know, I heard that the first thing on a woman's body that starts to go is the back of her arms. I figure that's why God put them where we couldn't see them."

Jane nearly toppled over laughing. When she finally caught her breath, she said, "I've noticed something else. I'm getting arm muscles. Look. *But pull over first!*"

Shelley obligingly did so. "Whaddya know. You *are* getting muscles."

"I like them," Jane said. "I thought we might drop in somewhere that I could buy some hand weights so I can keep them in both arms."

"Hand weights! You're going to exercise! I never thought I'd see the day!"

"Maybe we could even join one of those health clubs and both get back in shape," Jane burbled.

Shelley stiffened up and threw the car in gear. "That's going all too far! Exercising . . . ugh," she said with a shudder, and then said, "Look what Paul gave me last night." She dug in the center console and handed Jane a tiny phone.

"What's this for?"

"Calling while I'm driving."

Jane put her head in her hands and pretended she was sobbing. "Even safe drivers are a menace when they drive and talk on the phone. Promise me you'll never use it when I'm with you."

"Who would I be calling except you?" Shelley said. "And if I'm with you, I don't need to call you and you wouldn't be home, you'd be with me."

As Jane was deciphering this reasoning, they passed a fast-food restaurant and Shelley turned in to get a cup of coffee to go. Jane chose a huge glass of iced tea because the day was rapidly turning hot. They reached the community center and she had to shift her attention to exiting the van and walking up the stairs, balancing her heavy paper cup in her free hand. She only slopped a little of it down her leg.

They were early and only Stefan was already in the room. Jane looked over her notes from the previous day while the others wandered in. Within ten minutes, the adult students were ready for the day's topic. But the teacher hadn't appeared. They chatted among themselves for fifteen minutes. Jane took the opportunity to thank Arnold again for the beans. "I didn't even wait for today. I tried them out last night and they're delicious."

Arnie just looked pleased and nodded his head.

163

Ursula, stepping on a comb she'd dropped that looked like it was meant for currying a horse, leaped in. "A bean dish? Oh, do tell me the recipe. I love beans."

Jane whispered to Shelley, "Have you got that phone on you?"

"In my purse."

"Then pretend you're helping me to the bathroom and we'll call Mel and report that Eastman's still missing."

"Excuse us for a moment," Shelley said to the group. "Jane needs a helper."

"You call him," Shelley said, handing the phone to Jane when they reached the bathroom. "You just push the power button, wait a moment, then dial and push the button marked 'talk.'"

Jane fumbled with the tiny buttons and reached Mel on the third ring. "I thought you should know Dr. Eastman didn't turn up in class this morning."

Shelley tried to put her own ear to the tiny speaker. Jane waved her away and listened intently to Mel.

When the conversation was over and Shelley showed her how to hang up the phone, Jane said, "I'll tell you what he said when we're in your van. Meanwhile, just follow my lead."

They went back to the classroom and Jane said to the group, "Since Dr. Eastman has apparently been delayed, I suggest we go on with our tour planned for today. He had the list of addresses and can catch up with us later."

Ursula enthusiastically seconded this, and so did Miss Winstead, and the ladies left the room, leaving the men no choice but to follow.

As soon as Jane and Shelley were in the van and heading for Stefan's home, Jane reported that Mel had said the young boy at Eastman's house had called him early this morning. "The boy had gone to the garage to get a part to repair a garden-hose connection and discovered that Eastman's car was still there."

"So much for his driving upstate to his other property," Shelley said, as she uncharacteristically stopped at a yellow light.

"Mel thinks it's too coincidental that the first teacher of the class was attacked and the second teacher has disappeared."

"So, against all logic, it might involve someone in the class?"

"He didn't go as far as saying that. It's just something he's considering more significant than it seemed before."

"What are the police doing to try to find Eastman?"

"I didn't ask and he didn't mention it," Jane replied. "We have to pretend to ourselves we don't know any of this on the tour."

Stefan's yard was as boring as Jane's had been before she hired plants. But it wasn't nearly as messy. He apparently didn't have pets. There was a fairly small maple tree in the center of the grassy yard, and little scattered innocuous shrubs around the edges. This was a recently developed neighborhood and this appeared to be the way all the homes had been parsimoniously landscaped.

Almost everyone had suggestions. Miss Winstead's were the most sweeping. She suggested terraces, hidden garden rooms, and the pool having the water supply come out a hill. Just like her garden, of course.

Charles Jones argued for the opposite approach. Specimen plants on islands of mulch, so that each could be admired for its own special quality of growth and bloom. Geometric paths. Just like his garden.

Ursula said, "Just fill it up with plants you like and see what thrives and what dies and replace the dead ones with something else you'd like to try."

Poor Stefan tried to be polite about the suggestions, but still insisted that all he really wanted at first was a nice little pool with a fountain with some kind of sculpture spouting water in the middle and easy-to-grow, pretty flowers around the pool.

Miss Winstead launched into a treatise on caring for a pool, which was largely discouraging, even though she claimed to love hers. Shelley suggested that instead of making planting beds, Stefan could get mobs of nice planters to surround the pool and change the plants with the seasons.

Jane managed to drag Stefan away for a moment and say, "Wait till you see what I have on my patio. It might be a modest start for you."

He looked so grateful that she was afraid he'd be disappointed when he saw her little birdbath fountain.

Or maybe after Miss Winstead's lecture, he'd be happy to know he could have the lovely sound of running water surrounded by plants with very little trouble and work.

Only Arnold Waring was content to just roam around and examine the shrubs and not offer any advice at all or join in the competition for Stefan's approval of their own garden tastes.

Stefan finally got tired of advice and urged them along to Arnold's. When Shelley and Jane arrived, Shelley said, "I didn't realize Arnold lived so close to Julie Jackson's. Just across the street and three houses down."

"Hmm," Jane said. "I wonder if anyone questioned the neighbors after they found Julie. Old people on their own often keep an eagle eye on the houses around them. Arnold might have seen someone hanging about her house."

"I'm sure the police thought of that," Shelley said. "My goodness, Arnold keeps his house tidy. You can almost smell the fresh paint on the shutters."

"This iced tea has gone straight through me," Jane complained. "Would you run me home to pee?"

"Pee here. Well, not *right* here. I'm sure Arnold has a bathroom."

"I don't like asking."

"Jane, don't be frumpy. Don't you know everybody pees now and then? With your background, you've probably peed in fifteen or twenty different countries in strangers' houses."

"And I never liked to," Jane said with a laugh.

As they drove up to Arnie's house, Shelley noticed Geneva Jackson and her husband come out of Julie's house with a suitcase. "Only one suitcase?" she said. "I thought they were staying until Julie was out of the hospital."

Shelley waved and Geneva spoke to her husband, and he put the case in their car while Geneva came up the street briskly. "We're on our way to the hospital to bring Julie home!" she said with a huge smile. "The doctor thought it would be a couple days more, but she's making such improvement, and with a brother-in-law who's a neurologist staying with her, her physician is releasing her early."

Jane thought that was good news, but if she didn't find a bathroom soon, she'd create a scene.

Twenty-two

Jane said timidly, "Arnie, may I use your bathroom? I just drank a huge cup of iced tea."

"I saw you doing that. You're really making improvement moving around. The bathroom on the first floor doesn't have a door right now. I have a carpenter replacing it tomorrow, but there's another upstairs. Do you need help with the steps?"

Even if she had, she would have lied. The idea of a man taking her clear to the bathroom door didn't appeal to her. "No, I've practiced and I can make it by myself, thanks." She realized that even changing a door must be a wrench to Arnie. After all, his late wife must have touched that door thousands of times.

She made it up without any trouble at all for the first time. Visiting the very feminine bathroom—pink towels, little shell-shaped soaps that were so dusty they must have been there since the day Darlene died, a sparkling clean tub, old but freshly washed and ironed frilly pink curtains—she realized the full extent of his obsession. Even an old-fashioned rouge tin was sitting on the sink counter.

She glanced out the bathroom window. Everyone was assembled in Arnie's backyard. Everyone but Dr. Eastman. As she exited the bathroom, she noticed the bedroom doors to each side were open and couldn't resist just peeking, without going in them.

The one to the right was lovely but a bit cluttered. There was a gardening book with a bookmark in it on one of the night tables. A sparkling green water carafe with the equally clean glass turned over the top. The carafe was sweating slightly. Did Arnie really refill it with ice water every day for Darlene?

The bedspread was dark floral patterns with wide green stripes. Very neat, but very faded. The matching pillows were piled at the headboard. The one on what Jane assumed was Darlene's side was still a deep green. Arnie's was faded.

Dear Lord, he still had her pillow exactly as she'd left it all those years ago!

When Jane's husband died so ignobly, one of the first

things she did was get rid of the bedding and pillows and treat herself to something *she* liked. What a difference.

She stepped carefully to the other side of the small hall and glanced in what probably was once the guest room, now an office with a computer and desks and bookshelves. She was tempted to go in and see what the titles were, but resisted the impulse. She didn't want to be *that* snoopy.

This room obviously had few reminders of the wife. It was probably the only part of the house that was really Arnie's own turf. There were a couple of awards of some kind on a shelf, several blurred news clippings with pictures of firefighters in action on the bulletin board, and the same kind of paintings on the walls. A pile of paperwork with colored folders sticking out here and there was next to the computer. There was an old-fashioned brass stand ashtray by a butt-sprung leather chair with a reading light behind it. One cigar butt was in it. This was probably the only place Arnie smoked.

It's none of your business, she told herself fiercely as she headed back down the steps.

At least she was cheered by the fact that one room was strictly Arnie's and apparently well used. It seemed he actually had a few interests of his own. The computer, the memories of his life as a firefighter. Maybe he went out from time to time to visit old comrades or drop by the fire station itself and tell stories to the young men and women about the "good old times."

Or cook some of their meals from his wife's recipes.

She glanced in the living room as she passed. An old television, a rocking chair with a pink sweater still hanging over one arm, a half-finished afghan spilling from a bright yellow bag of yarn by the side. *Oh, Arnie,* she thought. *Let her go, please let her go.*

She passed through the kitchen to the back door without even looking at what treasures of Darlene's were still there, except to accidentally notice a row of little ceramic pots on the windowsill with struggling, leggy violets with yellowing leaves.

Arnie was standing outside the kitchen door when she opened it. "Did you make it okay up and down the stairs?"

Jane was determined to be cheerful. "I only bashed out three of the banister rails with my crutch. Just kidding. I didn't break anything."

She joined the rest of the group, hoping to prove to herself and the others that she could get around perfectly well. Arnie's garden was truly pathetic, even though there were signs of hard work going into it. A wheelbarrow sat at the edge of the patio with garden tools. A large sturdy wastebasket was bulging with weeds. But the poor plants were a mess. The gardens had probably been wonderful five or six years ago, but were as dusty and preserved as almost everything she'd seen in his home.

"You must divide the perennials, Arnie," Miss Winstead was saying. "Start with those Japanese irises. I'm astonished they've survived without division. They grow the first year out of one bunch of tubers and put next year's growth outside the circle of the plant. That's why all the clumps have holes in the middle. Take them up, cut the tubers in pie-shaped pieces, take out the dead middle, and start them over in well-turned soil."

"But that's where my wife wanted them," he objected.

"Of course," Miss Winstead said as authoritatively as always. "But take them out, cut them up, work in some compost and peat, and put a few of them back in and give the rest to friends. Do that every third year and they'll thrive."

Arnie looked questioningly at the irises. Jane assumed he was wondering if this plan could possibly fit in with his plans to honor his wife's garden. Jane hoped so.

She wandered around a bit, trying to keep up with the others as they moved around the perimeter of the yard where all the gardens were. Darlene had obviously loved bachelor buttons, and Arnie had let them self-seed for years. Poor things were leggy and the colors had cross-bred into murky light purples and blues, unlike fresh seeds with their vivid colors.

A huge peony bush that was finished blooming was falling away from its center, though Arnie had tried to prop up the desperate yellowing foliage with little green sticks. She mentally repeated Miss Winstead's advice to dig it up and divide it. Even Jane knew that was what you did with a peony that had run amok.

Piles of old bark mulch lined a cement path and looked as if they'd crumble to dust if stepped on or even touched. Some unidentifiable straggle of plants with stingy foliage and pitiful little faded coral pompom like flowers were struggling along in the ancient bark.

Miss Winstead was lecturing Arnie again toward the back of the yard. "Those would be beautiful white lilies if you divided them as well. They've crowded themselves almost to death and you've let a tree grow here that shades them. They like lots of sun. See that one over there that managed to self-seed itself into a patch of light? That one's perfection."

"That's the same kind of lily I sent Dr. Jackson," Stefan said, strolling up to Arnie and Miss Winstead. "I'd almost forgotten I did that. I wonder if her sister got the arrangement."

Shelley and Jane suddenly locked gazes of astonishment.

Stefan seemed to be admitting that he sent the flowers with the threatening note that was accidentally delivered to Jane's house the morning Julie was attacked. Shelley slipped away casually to the front of the house with her tiny cell phone in her hand, glancing back only once and nodding at Jane.

Jane had the urge to question Stefan, but knew Mel would have a stroke if he learned of her interference. She frantically asked Miss Winstead if the lily in question had a name.

"I imagine it's Casa Blanca. Just smell it. It has a

173

divine fragrance. Watch your step, Jane. You nearly fell into the hostas. Aren't the stamens spectacular. Such a good yellow-orange."

Jane remembered trying to get that color off her face when she and Shelley were taking the flowers to Dr. Julie Jackson's house.

Stefan suggested that maybe they could fit Mrs. Nowack and Mrs. Jeffry in today since they started so early in the day. Shelley and Jane were appalled. "Oh, no!" Shelley exclaimed. "I have to take a bunch of teenage girls to their cooking lessons. And Jane has an appointment. That's why we were so glad to be able to do the tours early."

Jane was nodding and feeling a bit as if she looked like Dr. Eastman's housekeeper, bobbing in agreement. But she was thinking frantically that Mike hadn't even mowed the yard yet and Willard had been out there since the last poop scooping.

Sensing that this was adjournment, everyone thanked Arnie and Stefan for letting them come see their gardens and moved in a disordered clump to the front of the house—just as a police car and a little red sports car stopped in front of Arnie's house. Mel got out of the car and a large uniformed officer lumbered out of the police vehicle.

Arnie was standing on the porch, waving good-bye to everyone, when he spotted the two interlopers and grabbed the porch rail to steady himself.

"Are you Arnold Waring?" Mel asked.

"Yes."

"And is one of your guests Stefan Eckert?"

Arnie pointed a shaking finger toward Stefan, who realized they were looking for him. He strolled over and said, "Have I parked in a place I shouldn't?"

"No, we would just like to ask you some questions. Would you mind coming with us?"

Stefan only looked slightly alarmed. He was more confused than scared. "May I ask what this is about?" But even as he spoke, he was moving obediently toward the cars in front.

"Not here, I think."

Stefan was invited to sit in the back of the police car, and both it and Mel's moved off.

Jane turned around and saw Arnie sitting on the porch with his head in his hands. "Arnie looks ill," she said, and they all rushed forward to give aid and comfort.

"Leave me alone," Arnie said when Miss Winstead asked him to raise his head so she could look at his pupils. Jane didn't quite understand this order. Did Miss Winstead suspect a stroke and were pupils a sign?

"You're as white as a ghost. You aren't well," Miss Winstead insisted.

"I'm not sick," Arnie insisted. "Just sick at heart. Imagine how upset poor Darlene would have been if the police had come to her garden and taken someone away."

Jane put her hand on his shoulder and spoke softly but firmly. "Darlene didn't see it, Arnie. She's not here.

175

She's not upset. Nor should you be. It had nothing to do with you or your late wife."

Color started coming back to his face and he struggled to his feet shakily. "You're right, Miss Jeffry. I was thinking of Darlene more than usual because it's really her garden I invited all of you to see."

"We know how you feel, Arnie," Jane said, though she really didn't understand him. "But you would honor Darlene best if you brought her garden back to what it once was by taking all the good advice you got today. You need to get out with a sharp shovel and some knives to divide plants, and I'll bet you'll have her garden back just like it once was by next spring."

Arnie stared at Jane for a long moment. "You may be right," he said before opening his front door. Slowly he went into the house and closed the door very gently.

Twenty-three

"I shouldn't have said that to him, about Darlene being gone," Jane lamented on the way home. "I think I hurt his feelings and all I meant to do was calm him down. He looked so terrible."

"I don't see why. For one thing, what you said was true. And the poor old guy could have had a heart attack or stroke thinking about what his wife would have felt if the police came into her yard. He doesn't even know if that's accurate. She might have gotten a kick out of it," Shelley said. "Keep in mind that we didn't know her."

Jane said, "While I was upstairs at Arnie's, I peeked in the two bedrooms."

"Of course you did," Shelley said. "Anybody would."

"But only from the open doorways," Jane amended, as if this counted toward a reputation for good manners. She described the bedroom, the ice water and carafe on Darlene's side of the bed, the pillowcase that had never been washed. The rouge tin on the vanity. The half-done afghan and sweater on Darlene's chair in the living room.

"I guess I'm not as softhearted as you. I think that's ridiculous," Shelley said.

"But very, very sad, too. I simply can't imagine wanting to live with a dead person, no matter how much I might have loved them when they were alive. My grandmother once had a friend who did that with her son's room. He died as a child and the room stayed exactly as it was the last time he left it for about forty years. It upset the mother every time she looked in, but she kept it that way anyhow. And the other children resented it enormously. They were all younger and had never even known the dead older brother. Even when they were adults and came to visit, nobody was allowed to set foot in that room, let alone sleep there. My mother's friend was unhappy all her life."

"I've heard stories like this before. I can't grasp why people would do that. Have you ever seen that commercial where the parents are bidding a tearful farewell to their college-graduate son, and the moment he's out of sight, Mom is measuring his room for where the new hot tub can go?"

"I laugh every time I see it," Jane replied. "And keep thinking about Mike's room. I want to turn it into my office the minute he graduates so I don't ever have to go back in the basement. I'll make the extra bathroom upstairs the laundry room when all three kids are gone. Speaking of Mike being gone, he hasn't mowed the lawn yet."

"Don't look at me," Shelley said. "I've made my life's work not knowing a thing about the way a lawn mower works. And I'm also too stupid to understand the fuse box."

"Nobody believes that."

"True. But it's my story and I'm sticking to it."

When they got home, Shelley's lawn service was tearing around her yard, using a wide variety of noisy machines. "Want me to loan them to you? Just this one time?"

"I can't afford it if we're going to buy me a television."

"I forgot about the television. How could I? Let's do that now, shall we? We'll drop the girls off at their cooking lesson first. When Mike gets home, he and a couple friends can haul it upstairs for you. And I warn you I won't let you be stingy about it. You need a nice big one with all the bells and whistles. Don't look at me that way, Jane. I know what I'm talking about. The first television we got for the bedroom was tiny and we had to sprawl in bed on our stomachs with our heads at the wrong end to see the picture."

Shelley was true to her word. Jane came home with a box that nearly filled half the back of Shelley's van. The van also contained a new VCR and a cabinet to put everything on.

"I wish we could haul it out now," Jane said.

"We couldn't do that if we had six women friends to help. It's one of those manly things to move televisions and furniture."

They went first to look over Shelley's yard. Freshly mowed, it looked and smelled wonderful. "What's that vine with the trellis in the big pot?" Jane asked.

Shelley walked over and pulled out a tag stuck in the soil. "Brugmansia, it says. Look at the picture."

"Good Lord! Those yellow flowers are gorgeous. The size of a child's head."

"And it's wonderfully fragrant. I saw them once in a Southern California hotel courtyard. They grew clear up to the second-story balcony and smelled divine."

"Southern California? That must mean you have to take it inside in the winter."

"I'll make Paul do that," Shelley said smugly.

"I wonder how Stefan's doing," Jane said, gesturing for Shelley to come along inside Jane's house. "I need a snack."

"Stefan probably isn't a happy camper, I'd guess. And he's going to be angry that somebody tipped off the police that he was the one who sent the flower arrangement to Julie. He's sure to make the connection to one of us."

"But he won't know which one of us, will he?" Jane hadn't thought of this before and it made her feel like a busy-mouthed tattletale even though Shelley actually made the call.

"Not unless Mel tells him."

"He wouldn't, I'm sure. He tells us things he probably shouldn't because he knows we'll honor his confidence. I'm positive he'll do the same thing for us. Stefan will probably blame the cops themselves for finding out. Or the florist. Or Miss Winstead."

"Stefan didn't look as upset as I expected when they took him away," Shelley said, rummaging in the bottom drawer of Jane's refrigerator looking for cold soft drinks.

"Nor did he seem to feel guilty when he told us. If he were guilty of something, he wouldn't have blurted out that he sent the flowers."

"Unless he'd come up with an innocent explanation in the meantime. Why don't you ever keep real Coke in here? I don't like the diet version."

"I do keep it and I drink it all. I'm sure there's at least one can left," Jane said.

Just then the telephone rang. It was Mel, and Jane listened carefully for a long time before saying, "Thanks for letting us know. You didn't tell him it was Shelley and me that ratted, did you?"

"What! What?" Shelley asked when Jane hung up.

"They've let Stefan go. He claimed effectively that he'd just written the note saying 'you're next' because she was the most highly qualified teacher scheduled for the next week's classes. He paid cash for the flowers because it wasn't something he could claim on his job expenses. Mel said he seemed so sincere that no one could doubt him. But there was another connection he also blabbed about without even being asked. Apparently he had been one of Julie's 'escorts' for her charity do's last year. He thought at first she was inviting him to them because she liked him, but he claimed he soon realized it wasn't romance she wanted, just a presentable man."

"Isn't that a suspicious story? Maybe he was heart-broken when he realized."

"Mel said he admitted it freely and with no sign of emotional involvement."

"Mel must be pretty naive to buy that, or maybe Stefan's a better actor than we could have guessed," Shelley said.

"Now who's being cynical and grumpy? You know Mel wouldn't turn him loose and forget all about him if he wasn't absolutely sure the guy was telling the truth. Mel's job is to not believe anything he's told until it's confirmed. He said they took him down to the florist shop for the owner to identify him. And Stefan didn't bat an eye."

Shelley shrugged. "Okay, okay. Stefan is very good-looking and I can see him dropping Julie when he realized he was just her boy toy. Other women have probably treated him the same way and he might have even been flattered, but got bored with the hoity-toity charity gang. I've been to my share of them with Paul and they're pretty deadly."

Mike came in the house as she was saying this. "What's deadly?" he asked.

"Me," Jane said.

Before she could launch into a few remarks about mowing the grass, Mike said, "What are all those big boxes in your car, Mrs. Nowack?"

"Your mother's new gigantic television, a VCR, and a table to put it on."

"Mom! You sprung for all this in one day? Have you gotten an inheritance you didn't tell us about? Some mysterious rich great-uncle you never told us about?" Mike asked.

"I just took it out of *your* inheritance," Jane said with a grin. "I deserve this stuff. I want to be a lady of leisure before it's too late. Call Scott and get him to help you carry it upstairs, would you? And I really need the lawn mowed."

"That's why I came home early. You knew I wouldn't forget. I'll even get Willard inside so he doesn't bark me to death. By the way, I brought home a couple bags of nice little river rocks so we can put them in Willard's path and make it look like it was a gardening choice."

"Mike, you are a wonder!" his mother said.

"So are you going to buy me my own television?"

"No," Jane said succinctly.

Mike looked as if he was slightly put out. Jane wondered if she'd seriously spoiled her kids by always putting them first and scrimping on her own needs. It must have been a surprise to him to find her spending money on herself for a change.

But Mike did a terrific job with the yard, and the path almost looked like a good idea. To Jane, at least. Willard checked it out and decided it was a dangerous demarcation he didn't dare cross. "He'll cut a new path," Jane said dismally. "We'll end up with concentric rings of paths in the grass."

Shelley was sitting down in the yard, examining the rocks. "This looks nice, Mike. Maybe later in the summer you can design a path for me with these rocks." She glanced at her watch and said, "I better go fetch the girls. I wonder what horror they learned to cook today."

Mel called while Scott, Mike's best friend, and Mike were struggling to carry the television up the stairs. Jane almost didn't answer the phone. She was too busy driving the boys insane with her warnings to be careful, not to drop the TV, or let the corners make dents in the wall, or hurt themselves.

"Jane, I'm sorry to tell you this, but you'll see it on the evening news and I thought you should know in advance."

She went cold, then hot all over. "What's happened?" she asked in a shaky voice. Her first thought was that Shelley had finally had the car accident Jane had anticipated for twenty years and she and the girls

183

were all in a hospital.

"It's nothing personal. Don't worry. I didn't mean to scare you. It's just that we found Dr. Eastman."

The silence that followed this was frigid. But Jane had to ask, "Is he all right?"

"No. He's dead. He'd been put in the compost pile that's hidden behind that stand of pines in his backyard. Fortunately a neighbor reported an awful smell, and the little boy and his mother weren't the ones that found him."

Jane made a hearty sigh of relief. "I should be sorrier than I am. I hardly knew the man. I'm just glad it wasn't something awful about Shelley and Katie."

"I'm really sorry I frightened you, Janey."

"How did he die?"

Mel paused. "Do you really want to know?"

"I guess so."

"He was strangled to death with a tough green twine that he used to tie up plants."

Twenty-four

"Omelettes!" Shelley said when she returned from picking up their daughters from the cooking class. "They learned how to make omelettes today. At least it was something more reasonable than a fancy chicken dish. Jane? Are you listening?"

"I have something to tell you, but not with kids swarming the house. Come look at my television first."

Mike and Scott had gotten it all set up and were lounging on Jane's bed, watching a movie of highly doubtful taste. They frantically flipped to a news channel when Jane and Shelley entered the room.

Shelley clasped her hands and exclaimed, "Isn't that wonderful? Terrific reception. A huge picture. And the cabinet looks great in here. Aren't you glad you decided to do this, Jane?"

"I'm not sure. There's going to be a big temptation to never get out of bed."

"Let's go outside while Mike and Scott dispose of all the rubble. Boys, put all the instructions and warranties in the drawer of the cabinet."

Mike rolled his eyes. "We'd have never thought of that," he said with sarcasm, softened with a smile.

Shelley was so anxious to hear what Jane had to say that she carried Jane's iced tea out to the patio for her without being asked. Held the back door open for her. Even fluffed up the patio chair cushion.

When they were settled in where their conversation couldn't be overheard, Jane said, "Mel called while you were gone. They've found Eastman. He's dead."

"No! You don't mean this!"

Jane repeated what Mel had told her.

"That's awful. And it really does point to someone in the class. I wouldn't have believed it," Shelley said.

"How do you figure that?"

"Two teachers of the same class in a row, Jane. One violently attacked, the other killed. You can't ignore the connection. And neither can the police."

"But, Shelley, all of the class are pretty normal pleasant people."

"Not exactly. You and I are normal pleasant people, but Charles Jones is an ironing board, Miss Martha Winstead had a long bitter history with Eastman and made no bones about it. And Ursula is a nutcase. And so is Arnie in a different way."

"You're right about Miss Winstead. But she's a tiny thing and old. Can you see her overpowering a large man, then hoisting him bodily into a compost bin? And as far as we know, she had nothing against Julie Jackson."

"We don't know that. She knew a lot about Julie and followed her social life in the papers. She might have disliked Julie Jackson as much as she hated Eastman and had the sense to keep quiet about it."

"Maybe. But it still seems physically impossible that she could do it. She's tough-minded, but little and frail. You heard her explain that she has hired men to do the heavy work in her yard. It's not that she's been bulking up by hauling tons of those rocks around herself."

"What about Arnie then?" Shelley suggested.

"That doesn't play. He's very strange, I admit. And probably strong for his age, having once been a fire-fighter. They have to be fit. But his obsession has nothing to do with either teacher. He can't think about anything except his late wife and trying to pretend she's still alive. He doesn't appear to have any connection with either of the teachers."

"Charles Jones?"

"He comes to our minds because we don't like him, Shelley. He's so stuffy, prim, and dull, but that doesn't mean he's hateful enough to knock someone off. Eastman didn't even make criticisms of Jones's garden. In fact, Eastman seemed to be the only one who slightly approved of Charles's style of gardening."

"But we have no idea what other relationship Charles and Dr. Eastman might have had, completely outside of gardening tastes."

"They didn't appear to have ever met."

"But maybe they were both concealing their acquaintance for some reason," Shelley said like a dog with a delectable bone to chew on.

Jane gave Shelley her due. "Charles Jones is a cold fish, I admit. A rigid perfectionist from what we've seen of his house and yard and his perfectly ironed and spit-polished personal appearance. And he's not very pleasant. He was complaining to me about Ursula and her garden. Swore there were ticks in her yard and wouldn't set foot beyond the patio. He isn't the least bit likeable, but I just don't see him doing something— anything—in a fit of passion. I don't see him as having the least passion about anything."

"Jane, just remember his garden. He's a very controlling person. Especially in the way he tortured and isolated those plants," Shelley said, getting up and jingling her car keys. "Think about this while I take the girls to the grocery store and show them how to buy eggs that aren't cracked or have dirty shells. They need to know about salmonella."

Jane propped up her bad foot on a chair and thought about what Shelley said. From their limited knowledge of the class members, none of them was strictly normal. Ursula led the pack in sheer personality disorder. Could she have developed some loony theory that Julie Jackson and Stewart Eastman were part of a dangerous conspiracy that she had to eliminate? It was certainly possible given her bizarre beliefs.

And she was a big woman. If she'd dug up and hauled around those tombstones in her garden by herself, she was strong enough to wrestle a body into a compost bin. On the other hand, she was perpetually cheerful and up front with her views and didn't seem to take the least offense when someone doubted that she was right. And her tending to Jane had been a kindness, however useless and unsolicited.

Jane often prided herself on being able to pierce the veil of people's personalities, but she was striking out this time. She'd spent more time with Ursula than she'd wanted or needed, but still had no idea what really made her tick.

Nor could she figure out Charles Jones. He was a stiff, cranky, overorganized man. Something of a prig, in fact. But what kind of concealed life he might have was entirely unknown to her. He might secretly love Mozart or Jackson Pollock. He could have a sexy lover of either sex. He could be a rabid right-wing fanatic or a secret agent for the Nazi underground. Who could guess what was under that haughty, prim facade?

As for Miss Martha Winstead, she was just as much of a mystery. Had she ever married? Had children? Traveled? What was her background? And most of all, was her hatred of Stewart Eastman legitimate? There was always another side to any story, and maybe his actions had been justified. They'd never hear his version, though.

Miss Winstead's beloved cousin, whom she'd characterized as so meek and sweet, might have actually been a tartar of a woman who was set on dragging her husband's career into the dust out of sheer stupidity or spite. Even the account of his serving divorce papers on her when she was ill could be an exaggeration or even downright untrue. They'd only heard Miss Winstead's highly colored account of the marriage.

Miss Winstead had a steel spine, was highly opinionated, and believed she was always right. And she was also a snoop, not that Jane hadn't done her own share of snooping. But Jane didn't share her gossip and opinions with strangers, only with Shelley. Miss Winstead told them a lot of gossip about the other classmates when she was virtually a stranger to Jane and Shelley.

Still, she was a little woman, probably in her mid-sixties at least, with those small knobby hands and thin arms. How could she possibly have overpowered two larger people?

Come to think about it, what did Julie Jackson and Stewart Eastman have in common? They were both in the plant business in a similar way. They both had local connections, though Eastman spent most of his time elsewhere. They were highly educated and apparently were respected in their fields of endeavor. And Julie Jackson had agreed to lecture, and Stewart Eastman had taken over the class for her.

Was someone suspicious of their relationship, or jealous? Could they have actually conspired against someone? Or did somebody mistakenly assume they had? Jane asked herself, but came up blank. Nobody but Miss Winstead and Charles Jones took gardening seriously. But they weren't entirely obsessed with it. Miss Winstead still volunteered at the library and read the papers and went to lunch with new acquaintances like her and Shelley. Charles had a job that had to do with computers, if Jane was remembering correctly.

Even Ursula had interests that went far beyond mere plants and flowers. Way beyond. Her little old ladies she periodically took care of. Her pets. Feeding birds. Reading every conspiracy book ever published.

And Arnie Waring wasn't the least interested in gardening. He didn't even know the basics. He was concerned only with maintaining his lost wife's life as if she were going to come back someday and chide him for forgetting her. He had only an obligation to plants, not a love of horticulture. And he apparently kept himself busy with a few other things. Cooking. Feeding what he assumed was an invalid. Presumably, working with his computer and maybe those papers on his desk had to do with some special interest he pursued.

Who did that leave? Only Stefan. He was connected

to Julie by having had a few impersonal dates with her. If he was telling the truth. And maybe he was. Mel was half-convinced that Stefan was open with them when questioned and even stupidly provided another motive for himself. He'd been the very picture of helpful innocence when Mel came to fetch him to the police station. As if he had nothing whatsoever to hide. Maybe Shelley was right that he was a fabulous actor, but Jane doubted it. He'd been clearly intimidated by Dr. Eastman on the first day of class. He hadn't been able to hide his feelings that day.

Mike and Scott finally abandoned the television and came out with the lawn mower and weed whacker and started making a lot of noise and a great show of being good kids working on the yard.

Jane stayed where she was, still brooding over the attack and the murder. Who was left to consider? No one.

Except Geneva Jackson and her husband.

They not only knew Julie well, but were related. And Jane had the impression that Geneva was well acquainted with Dr. Eastman as well.

Twenty-five

Shelley's daughter, Denise, Katie, and Katie's best friend, Jenny, produced a fine dinner that evening. They made little individual omelettes that were really good. Jane chose the one with chives and sour cream.

Shelley went for the crumbled bacon and chopped tomatoes. As per the cooking teacher's suggestion, they served a mixed-fruit dessert that was the perfect finish. Except for the tiny marshmallows they decided to add on their own. They were a bit slimy by the time the fruit was served.

Mike and his friend Scott had worked up considerable appetites working on the yard and consumed vast quantities of dinner.

"Don't supervise the cleaning up this time," Jane warned Shelley. "See if they remember to get to it on their own."

The two women were sitting in Jane's bedroom, feeling bloated and satisfied. Shelley was perched on the corner of Jane's bed. Jane was at the head of the bed with her bad foot propped up on a pillow. It had been a bit more painful this evening and she thought it needed a little pampering. They were watching a garden show.

"This guy is claiming he takes care of this ten-acre garden entirely on his own," Shelley said. "I don't believe him."

"I've been thinking over the members of the class," Jane said, not caring much whether the gardener on the show did his own work. It was the sort of thing only Shelley could get cranky about.

"And the murder?" Shelley asked.

"I sat outside while you were gone and ran down the list of suspects from the class. I could think of feeble motives for a few of them, none of which are very convincing. Then I got to Geneva and her husband. We've both forgotten about them. But they're the most likely. Most violent acts occur within families, I think. That's what Mel said."

"I've heard that, too," Shelley said. "What's your reasoning?"

"First, Geneva is Dr. Jackson's sister. Maybe they didn't get along. Perhaps there was a long-term hostility between them. And unless Julie has a child we don't know about or other siblings, Geneva is probably her heir."

"You think Julie Jackson is rich?"

"She must be if she's always going to these charity functions. You don't get invited if you haven't contributed wads of money and can afford to dress to the nines."

"I hadn't thought about it that way," Shelley admitted.

"And remember that Mel told us she had a lot of valuable knickknacks and expensive artsy stuff in her house and he was wondering why the person who came in her house didn't steal them."

"If it was Geneva or her husband who attacked her, they wouldn't have bothered to take anything away because it would come to them anyway if she died. I see where you're going. But why would they need her money? Geneva's husband is a neurology something. I'd imagine they make money hand over fist."

Jane shrugged. "Maybe he's not a very good one, or not in a good practice."

"But Geneva has a job as a trialler, it seems. At least that's the impression I got."

"I don't suppose you get rich doing that," Jane said. "And it must be a lot of work."

They sat in silence for a few minutes, watching the man on the television show brag about his extensive hosta garden and rare plants he grew. Shelley finally said, "There was something that crossed my mind a while ago. I think I mentioned it already. It's about Arnie. Lots of older people keep a close eye out for what's going on in their neighborhood. It seems to keep them alert to both danger and gossip. Did Arnie's office have windows at the front of the house?"

"Two large ones with an easy chair and a side table in front of them."

"So maybe he noticed something or somebody that didn't belong, or seemed suspicious but just hasn't put it together with the attack on Dr. Jackson."

"You're suggesting that we question him? Mel won't like that."

"He will if we prod a valuable memory out of him."

"What's our excuse for going to his house?" Jane asked, swinging her cast-bound foot off the bed.

"We'll take him the girls' recipes for the omelettes since he likes to cook. Maybe he'd like to branch out from Darlene's."

"I doubt it, but it is a good excuse."

Jane went downstairs to ask Katie to write up the recipe for the basic omelette and a list of possible fillings while Shelley went home to check her answering machine and freshen her makeup. Then they drove to Arnold Waring's house.

He greeted them with surprise and pleasure. He probably didn't get much drop-in company. "Come in, ladies. What are you up to?"

"We have a recipe to share with you. We'd have brought the actual food along with it except that omelettes don't travel well," Shelley told him.

He invited them into his living room and settled Jane in a comfy chair with an ottoman to put her bad foot on. He and Shelley sat on the long sofa across the front window. He looked over the recipe and said he'd try it and that it sounded good. Shelley was staring at the rocking chair with the half-finished afghan beside it and the pink sweater draped over the back.

Jane told Arnie about their daughters taking a cooking class. He liked this. "Most young women these days don't learn how to cook. They all go to restaurants or get take-out food. Darlene wouldn't have heard of doing that. You're doing the right thing for your daughters."

"Arnie . . ." Jane said hesitantly. "We want to ask you about something."

"Ask away, not that I'll know the answer. I wasn't as well educated as my wife."

"It's not an educational question, it's an observation thing. I imagine that, living alone, you keep a pretty good eye on what's going on around the neighborhood. Single people living alone really need to look after themselves. At least I feel that way when my kids are in school or away."

Jane hoped this was tactful wording and was glad when Arnie nodded agreement.

"With all the awful things that go on today, everybody must be wary," he said.

"Well, we were wondering, since you live so close to Dr. Jackson's house, whether you noticed anything odd the morning she was attacked."

There it was, out in the open. Jane held her breath, hoping he wasn't going to take offense at her suggesting he was nosy.

"The police asked me that the day they were around," Arnie said. "I guess they asked everyone on the block. I couldn't think of anything . . . then."

"But you've remembered something?" Shelley asked, trying not to sound too eager.

"It was just a car I hadn't seen before. An old one. A Ford, I think. Black or dark blue."

"Where did you see it?"

"Right in front of Dr. Jackson's house. I didn't really make anything of it at the time. She often has company."

"On the street or the driveway?" Jane asked.

"Oh, on the street. It might have been somebody visiting the house across from her, of course." He thought for a moment. "No, I guess not. Those folks were off on a trip to Disney World with their kids if I remember right. The kids brought back a pillow for me with a Mickey Mouse face last Sunday. Nice kids. Being raised right. They come over and I tell them stories of my days at the firehouse."

This warmed Jane's heart. It was lovely that a neighbor paid attention to old Arnie, and the kids liked him as well.

"So the car probably belonged to someone calling on Dr. Jackson? Don't you think that you should tell the police now that you've remembered it?" She was hesitant about even mentioning the police after Arnie's near fainting spell when they came to his—or rather, Darlene's—home.

"Maybe, but it wouldn't be much help. I'm not even sure it was a Ford, and it might have been black or dark blue. That wouldn't be of much use to them. There are probably thousands of cars like that."

"Still . . ." Jane urged.

"I don't want the police here," Arnie said.

"No, of course not," Shelley said brightly. "It makes talk around the neighborhood. But the detective who came here with the officer is a friend of Jane's, and her neighbors are used to seeing him around her house. Maybe you could drop by Jane's and talk to him there."

Arnie said, "I guess that would be okay. Maybe when we're touring your two yards tomorrow."

"I'll set it up. It'll only take you a minute to tell them about the car you saw. If it's not valuable information, they won't bother you again," Jane assured him.

"Okay. Now, if you have the time, I'd like you to come look at something."

He took them to the backyard and said, "I might take

Miss Winstead's advice about dividing these Japanese irises. She said to do it in the fall. But I'd like to put the cuttings somewhere else in the yard."

You won't do it, Jane thought, but went along with allowing the visit to last longer. She glanced around the yard again, and once again noticed the pitiful straggly plants with the little coral droopy pom-pom flowers. "Why don't you plant the extra cuttings over here?" she suggested. "The colors would go well together. And these little plants look like they're struggling for light. You could move them into the sunshine."

And the irises would kill off the ugly plants, she reflected.

Arnie nodded. And leaned down to pluck a few flowers off and handed a couple to both Jane and Shelley. "They don't look like much, but they smell nice. Darlene used to put the foliage in vinegar for salad dressing."

"That went well, I think," Shelley said when they were on their way home.

"I hope it's useful to Mel to know about this mystery car. Take me home now. I want to put on my jammies and veg out in front of my new television."

Twenty-six

The last day of the class was anticlimactic. Though the death of Dr. Eastman had been on the local evening news and there was even a mention of the suspicious circumstances, treated almost as a joke on one of the networks Friday morning, the class assembled at the community center dutifully.

All except Stefan.

He'd come to the classroom either the evening before or early in the morning. He left a note on the podium saying since one or more of the class attendees had reported an innocent remark he'd made the day before to the police, causing him much humiliation, he wouldn't be present today.

So he hadn't been as casual and unconcerned as he acted when he was taken away. Jane couldn't blame him a bit.

Everyone was subdued and feeling awkward in the presence of the others. Miss Winstead looked downright haggard and was the first to bring the subject out in the open. "What a perfectly horrible way to die," she said.

When no one else replied, she continued, "I had a long, highly unpleasant relationship with the man, but I wouldn't have wished this on anyone."

"It was a shame," Arnie contributed.

Geneva Jackson, who had come this morning now that her sister was comfortably settled back in her own home, murmured a vague agreement with Arnie.

"We're all under suspicion, you realize," Ursula said bluntly. "The police will pick one of us at random to persecute and perhaps even prosecute."

A bleak silence fell over the room and it grew darker by the coincidence of a storm front moving in front of the sun just as she spoke. Nobody bothered to turn on the lights.

"I think we should all just go home," Charles Jones said. "There's no point in finishing our tour or the class."

Shelley spoke up. "I disagree. Jane and I would welcome you to see our yards and give us the benefit of all your experience. We've been looking forward to you coming. And nothing will bring Dr. Eastman back. His death was a tragedy, of course, but none of us are quitters, I hope."

Remarkably, they were all so cowed by the situation and Shelley's remarks that they went along with what she said.

Charles Jones grudgingly agreed. "We'll have to make them short visits and put this all behind us."

"Not entirely put the experience out of our minds," Ursula said rather sensibly given her normally extreme views. "No matter what else happens, I for one have learned a great deal of useful information from the rest of you. And I agree that the last two gardens deserve to be seen."

It was turning into a bleak day, with the sky darkening and death discovered yesterday. Jane would have been perfectly content if they didn't come to see her yard, except for the fact that she'd called Mel late the night before and told him about the conversation she and Shelley had with Arnie and how he was willing to tell what little he'd observed, but only if he could meet Mel privately at Jane's house.

But secretly she was in agreement more with Charles Jones than with Shelley. A fine twist of fate. She'd rather go home and spend a day that threatened to become rainy and dark in her cozy, safe bedroom mindlessly watching her television than have all these people to her house.

She still wasn't entirely convinced, in spite of the coincidences, that the attack on Dr. Jackson and the murder of Dr. Eastman had been committed by one of the class. She recognized it was a possibility, but so were a lot of other scenarios that nobody but Mel was aware of.

But she couldn't betray Shelley's wishes and opt out. "Let's go to my house first and Shelley's after mine. Her yard is nicer than mine," she said as Shelley was jingling her car keys meaningfully.

The rest of them dragged themselves out of their chairs and followed Shelley and Jane to the parking lot. Everyone but Jane had driven their own cars, in anticipation, probably, of being free to bolt when they wished to.

When they all reassembled at Jane's house, she did her best to be cheerful and welcoming. She'd noticed Mel's little red MG parked up the street where he was waiting to tactfully pluck Arnie out of the crowd and have a talk with him. She doubted that Arnie's information would be helpful, but was in too deeply to back out.

Nobody had much to say about Jane's yard, although they all tried to be polite about her clearly recently imported plants around the patio in tubs. Ursula asked about the nice little rocks that covered Willard's damage to the yard. "It's an odd but appealing curve from one side of the yard to the other, but what are you planning to do next?" she asked with abnormal social grace.

"I thought I'd line both sides of the path with some low-growing ground cover," Jane improvised. "Can you suggest something suitable?"

"Let me think about it. I'll give some starts of several of my ground covers you could try out. It's a little late in the season to start them, but you might as well give it a try."

Out of the corner of her eye, she saw Mel signaling to Arnie, who moved unobtrusively and unwillingly toward him.

Miss Winstead caught Jane's attention and said, "I envy the view of the field behind your house. It's rare to find a big open area like that in a well-developed suburb."

This gave Jane the chance to explain how it had happened to be there. "It was the last block of houses in this division that were planned. The developer got in trouble with the financing of the building project, and for some reason nobody knows, a multitude of lawsuits have dragged out for years, preventing anyone else coming and building. The homeowners' society has taken over temporary responsibility for keeping it attractive. Part of our dues are spent on mowing it early in the spring and scattering wildflower seeds on it."

"What an excellent solution," Miss Winstead said.

"Over the last five years or so the wildflower plants seem to have finally beat out the weeds. Otherwise it would really be a blight," Jane agreed. She was blathering along on autopilot. "Frankly, I hope the lawsuits drag out for the rest of my life. I'd hate to lose this view. And my cats enjoy the field enormously. They'd be heartbroken if houses went up back there, and so would I."

Geneva had joined them and had been listening. She said, "Someone ought to write an article about this. It might be very encouraging to other communities that have open land that's left to be a blight."

Miss Winstead had been considering the view with head slightly tilted and eyes half-shut. "Jane, you know what would make this even better? If you replace that fence across the back of your yard with something rustic. A simple split-rail fence would fit in better with the wildness and beauty of the field."

As they left Jane's yard for Shelley's, Arnie slipped back into the group. Nobody seemed to notice he'd been missing. Jane was dying to speak to Mel, but didn't dare disappear.

Shelley had gotten their girls to cooperate with her

plans. An enormous pitcher of iced tea and a plate of tiny iced cakes were sitting out, lightly covered with plastic wrap. Colorful plates and glasses were ranged around her patio table.

"You just did this to show me up," Jane hissed.

"I did it to misdirect their attention from my store-bought garden," Shelley replied in a whisper.

No one was fooled. It was obvious to the real gardeners that Jane and Shelley's "gardens" had recently been trucked in. "You should keep these things," Ursula said, "instead of sending them back to the nursery."

"How did you know?" Jane asked with a laugh.

"They're too perfect and they're all in brand-new pots. But that's okay. You might learn some things by caring for them."

The group made serious inroads on the tea and cakes, until there was a flash of lightning and distant thunder. Threatening weather gave the guests a legitimate reason to flee.

"I've enjoyed meeting all of you," Shelley said hurriedly as everyone headed for their cars. This didn't seem an appropriate way to end a class, everyone running for cover and probably hoping they'd never meet again.

"That wasn't too bad," Jane said when they were all gone. "At least we showed that we cared about our yards enough to make an effort to spruce them up."

"They knew we cheated," Shelley said bluntly. "We should have done what Stefan did—let them see it in the raw and make suggestions."

When Jane went back to her house, she was surprised to see Mel still sitting at her kitchen table, eating a ham sandwich. "Sorry, but I've missed lunch for three days in a row. Hope you don't mind that I raided your refrigerator."

"Not in the least," Jane said, sitting down next to him. "Was Arnold Waring helpful?"

Mel shook his head. "Not at all. It was all so vague. He wasn't sure of the color, make, or age of the car he claims he saw in front of Dr. Jackson's house."

"Claims?"

"My instinct tells me he made it up," Mel said. "He's a lonely old man, wanting to look helpful and cooperative, I think. We'd already questioned everyone else on the block about strange vehicles or unfamiliar people on the street during the early morning of the attack on Dr. Jackson. Nobody could think of anything unusual."

"Maybe they were all just busy with their own lives and didn't notice," Jane said. It was a feeble excuse, but she felt honor-bound to make it.

"Jane, you know better," Mel said, grinning. "This kind of old neighborhood has people who keep an eye out for anything odd happening. You and Shelley are good examples."

Jane started to object to this characterization, but Mel put out his hands to stop her. "It's not a criticism. It's how neighbors are supposed to be. Looking out for each other."

"So you really think Arnie made up the suspicious car?"

"I do. But I'll get uniforms to go to every house again. There's about a one percent chance that someone else might have noticed this mystery car and will remember it when asked a second time."

"Or let their imaginations run away on them," Jane said.

"Exactly."

"Mel, you're looking so tired. Can't you get a little time off this case? Maybe we could go to a movie tonight."

"And let you thrash more innocent people with that crutch?"

Twenty-seven

Shelley hauled Jane around while taking the girls to their cooking class and they tried a little shopping while the storm passed, but Jane was so dangerous in a mall that they soon gave up the effort. But not before a sales clerk had patted Jane's arm and asked, "How did you do that to yourself?"

"I fell off the roof while I was cleaning gutters," Jane said.

"Why would you be cleaning gutters this time of year?" the clerk sensibly asked.

"Oh, I do it four times a year, rain or shine."

"Well, darling, don't do it again. There are people

you can hire for that."

"What's the next one you're going to try?" Shelley asked as they got back to the van.

"I don't know yet. I haven't tried skiing in the Alps yet, have I? Shelley, people like my fake answers better than the real one. When I say I fell off a curb, they immediately lose interest and think I was just clumsy."

"Which you were," Shelley said.

"What now?"

"I don't know," Shelley said, stopping a bare half inch from the car in front of them. She leaned on the horn. "She had plenty of room to get out if she'd just moved along with traffic. You know, I have a sense of anticlimax. The class is over. Neither the attack nor the murder is solved. Or near being solved. We've struck out, Jane."

"Not yet. Anybody but us surviving the class might have done the deeds."

"And a lot of other complete strangers, too," Shelley said, passing the car that had held her up and glaring fiercely at the hapless driver.

"I don't think so. The class was full of peculiar people."

"Everybody's peculiar in their own way. Look at Kipsy."

"You would bring her up."

"And you're peculiar yourself," Shelley went on. "Making up those loony stories about how you hurt your foot."

207

"But I'm just entertaining myself and others," Jane claimed. "It's a perfectly innocent thing to do. Makes everybody happy."

"Want to drop in on the cooking class?"

"Absolutely not. We'll learn soon enough what we're going to be subjected to tonight. I liked the omelettes, though. If Katie would just cook them once a week, I'd be happy to let her. I should probably be getting home. Mike's always stretching out the buttonholes on his knit summer shirts, and I promised I'd get to tightening them up for him this week. That's something I can do with no effort."

"I'm supposed to be calling everyone to set up the fall car pools this week, too," Shelley said. "Why do I always get stuck with that job?"

"Because you do it superbly well. And it helps that everybody's afraid to argue with you."

They parted in Shelley's driveway and Jane got upstairs to her sewing room quite efficiently and brought down Mike's shirt collection, and threads to match all the buttonholes. She settled in the living room and watched an old, and not top-rate, Katharine Hepburn movie while she sewed. But her mind was still on the events of the week. Why would anyone attack Julie Jackson and then murder her substitute teacher for the gardening class? Was it simply a hideous coincidence? She couldn't accept that it was. And Shelley was right that everyone in the class was rather off the norm.

Stiff, ultratidy Charles Jones certainly wasn't

normal. And he was cranky besides. Who knew what grudges he might have held for one or both of the teachers?

Neither was Martha Winstead normal. She was one of the toughest old ladies Jane had ever met. Normally, tough old ladies appealed enormously to Jane because she intended to be one someday, but for some reason Miss Winstead made her uneasy and she couldn't quite figure out why.

Ursula Appledorn was the weirdest of all. Kind but bossy. Smart but nutsy with conspiracy theories.

Arnold Waring was a nice old gentleman with a terrible obsession for keeping his dead wife's memory alive.

And she had no idea what made Stefan Eckert's mind work. He seemed so charming and pleasant on the surface, but came nearest guilt by having sent the flower arrangement to Julie with a message he claimed was innocent, but sounded guilty.

And who could guess what Geneva Jackson and her husband might be up to? They seemed the most likely to be the connection between Julie Jackson and Stewart Eastman. At least Julie, Geneva, and Stewart were in businesses that appeared to overlap. Could that be it? A business deal gone badly wrong? With Geneva the only one still standing and healthy? But strangely, Geneva seemed the most normal of the entire group of gardeners. Though she never spoke, that Jane could remember, of her own gardening tastes and was the only one not to attempt to force Stefan and Arnie to adopt her own tastes.

The kitchen door opened and Mel called out, as he had so often, "Why don't you *ever* lock your doors? I know you're here somewhere because Shelley's van's in her driveway." As he came into the living room, he exclaimed, "Dear God, that's such a domestic scene!"

"I'm only sewing buttonholes."

"Why did you never tell me? I could use some help with buttons," he said, sitting down next to her so her thimble disappeared between the sofa cushions.

"Are you through for the day? Want to reconsider going to a movie?" Jane asking, nipping off a loose thread and picking up the next shirt.

"No, just wanting to share some information with your overly fertile imagination. I checked out the class members as well as I could. Stefan Eckert was once arrested for striking a woman student."

"No!"

Mel shrugged. "Never came to court. The girl finally admitted that her boyfriend was the one who blacked her eye and she blamed Stefan because he was her faculty adviser and was disappointed at her choice of classes. And Miss Winstead wasn't quite telling you the truth about her hatred of Dr. Eastman. She took him to court when her cousin died. Apparently the cousin had inherited a lot of money from an aunt and didn't have a will, so the money went to Eastman. Miss Winstead dragged out a lawsuit for so long that he finally just gave her the money to get her out of his hair. He must have been making a lot of his own money by then."

"So much for an inheritance from an aunt," Jane said.

"Was that what she told you? Cagey old gal."

"What about Ursula?"

"A few unproven drug charges and two arrests after she was sent back from Vietnam for not quite following the rules as closely as the army thought she should. The report is very vague. She had an excellent reputation there as a nurse. So I don't know why she was sent home in spite of her objections."

"What about Charles Jones?"

"No blots on his record whatsoever except one late income tax payment."

"I thought he'd be the sort to send in his return early," Jane said, trying to fit a button into a buttonhole she'd made too small.

"And the old boy Arnie had lots of commendations from his job with the fire department. Credited for saving lots of lives. Said to work up a real adrenaline rush at fires and take chances others wouldn't."

"Somehow that doesn't surprise me," Jane said. "Say, Ursula wasn't taking care of Arnie's wife while she was dying, was she?"

"I have no idea."

Jane said, "Oh, well. It doesn't compute anyway. Nothing happened to either of them. Nor did either make any bad comments about the other. Never mind."

Mel got up and stretched. "Well, back to the salt

mines. You and Shelley apply your overactive imaginations to this information for a while. It'll keep you out of the pool halls."

"Probably not," Jane said. "I might learn to shoot pool with my crutch. Is that legal?"

"Probably not, but give it a shot. See you later. Lock your door." He gave her a slightly more serious kiss than the last time before he left.

Jane was done with the shirts and decided to do what little cleaning she could in the kitchen before the girls started their dinner project. She scared the cats out of the house, trying to wield a floor mop and one crutch. Willard moved into the far end of the living room and woofed pitifully.

She managed to knock over Arnie's flowers, but without breaking the little vase she'd put them in. She also made a tiny dent in the refrigerator door and almost toppled over a kitchen chair. And it didn't look any better when she was done.

Her hands felt sticky and she smelled them.

And a light dawned. Feeble, but a flicker of understanding took fire.

Twenty-eight

Jane sat down in the living room, turned off the television, and just thought for a long time. Pieces started falling in place. But only if she was right about what she was remembering. She'd been a little obsessed with her foot all week, just like poor old Arnie was obsessed. Maybe she would be as weird as he was if she had to wear the cast for the rest of her life.

It could be anyone, but the one she was thinking about could fit all the requirements if the things she'd seen—and smelled—were right.

She could hardly wait for Shelley to return. Shelley would talk her out of this and she'd be glad. She went back to the kitchen where she could watch for the van to return. And waited. And waited. They must have been making another heavy hit at the grocery. God only knew what they'd fix for dinner tonight.

Shelley came in with a bag of groceries. "Only dessert tonight. Black Forest cake. Had to stop at the liquor store to get Cherry Heering. I've never heard of it."

"We're only eating dessert?"

"No, I'll make a salad and rolls for dinner."

"Come outside. I need to run something by you. In private."

She started by telling Shelley what Mel had said he'd found out about the rest of the class.

"Nothing really there, is there?" Shelley said.

"But while I was tidying the kitchen, I noticed a smell."

"Lysol, probably."

"No. Smell my hand."

"Do I have to?" Shelley sniffed delicately and asked, "Eucalyptus?"

"Nope. Guess again. Close your eyes."

Shelley sniffed again, eyes closed. "Oh, I know. So what?"

Jane explained.

Shelley objected to every step of Jane's theory, as Jane thought she would.

But Jane said, "All we need to do is make a short visit to Julie's house. A sympathy call. We'll take them some of the girls' cake after dinner. That might be a good get-well present."

"We hardly know her. And your idea is insane. They'll throw us out."

"But what if I'm right? Only Julie will know."

"Julie Jackson has amnesia, in case you've forgotten."

"Only about the attack on her. Mel says she remembers everything before she was hurt. And that's what we need to know."

Katie, Denise, and Jenny were already destroying the kitchen with their early stages of making the Black Forest cake. Jane tried to keep from watching what they were doing. She called Mel from her upstairs extension and confirmed that Julie remembered most things that happened before she was hurt.

"What have you got on your mind?" Mel asked suspiciously.

"Just a question and a look at her office. If I'm wrong, I'll shut up. Shelley is sure I'm wrong."

"Jane, don't do anything stupid, okay?"

"We won't be in the slightest danger. I promise."

Mike turned up for dinner. "How'd your garden tour go?" he asked.

"Everybody knew it was faked," Jane said.

"Have you seen what Katie and her friends have done to the kitchen? What are they making?"

"Black Forest cake. I'm afraid to see so much as a glimpse of the kitchen."

Mike loved the cake and so did the rest of them. The girls had even cleaned up the splattered batter and the smears of cherry juice they'd spilled down the front of a cabinet. It was a fight to keep Mike from finishing the cake up. Jane had to cut off three little token pieces to take to the Jackson house. Mike begged Katie to make it again over the weekend. "That will really impress Sandra," he said.

Jane resisted, with great restraint, asking who Sandra was. Had he ferreted out Kipsy's real name or was a new Sandra on the horizon?

She called ahead and asked Geneva Jackson if she and Shelley could drop by with a dessert. Geneva was delighted. "We had take-out barbeque for dinner, which we all pretty much hated. We'd love a dessert. I'll start a big pot of coffee."

Fortunately, Julie was back in her basement office when they got there. "I'll call to her to come up," Geneva said.

"Don't bother," Jane replied. "We'll go down to her."

When they got to the basement, Jane was pleasant

215

but brisk. "Dr. Jackson, I'm Jane Jeffry. We've met before."

"At the city hall flap about cats on leashes," Julie laughed.

"And this is Shelley Nowack, my next-door neighbor and best friend. We were enrolled in the class you were to give on botany and gardening. I have three questions to ask you if you don't mind."

Julie looked surprised. "I guess that's all right. I hope I can answer them."

"Okay. First, would you open one of your file drawers?"

Julie, looking a bit like she was concerned for Jane's mental health, pulled a drawer open. Jane nodded, thanked her, and asked the second question. "Here's a list of the people in the class. Do you recognize any of the names?"

Julie studied the list. "Most of them," she said.

"Have you done whatever you do, which I'm sorry I don't quite grasp, for any of them?"

"I was called in to analyze material regarding a patent for these two." She picked up a pencil and checked off two names.

Jane nudged Shelley. "I think I'm right. Thank you so much, Dr. Jackson. There's Black Forest cake and coffee upstairs. Are you feeling well enough to have some?"

Julie smiled. "After nearly five days of hospital food? Of course I am."

Jane and Shelley made small talk, knocked back a

cup of coffee each, and made their escape.

As soon as they were on their way home, Shelley said, "It isn't proof of anything."

"But there is proof. And Mel can get to it if it hasn't been destroyed yet."

Jane went straight home and called Mel and outlined her case. He, like Shelley, scoffed at her crazy reasoning. But having hashed it out with Shelley and squashed her objections, Jane was ready with her ammunition.

"Jane, I don't pretend to believe this story."

"But you'll check it out anyway."

"I guess I have to."

On Saturday, Jane was never away from the phone, but Mel didn't call. He'd either found a lead of his own, or was still chewing over what she'd said. She knew better than to run him down and ask which it was.

Sunday morning he called and said, "May I run by and take you for a ride? Maybe somewhere out in the country where you can't hurt anyone with your crutches?"

It was a rehearsed line. Meant to be funny, but failing.

She was ready and waiting outside when he drove up. She squashed herself into his little MG, being very careful not to dent it with the crutch. They were well out of town when he finally said, "You were right. He admitted all you imagined, and more."

"You probably won't believe me, but I'm sorry I was

217

right," Jane said sadly.

"You might not be when you hear all of it. You were right about the flowers he gave you. Dr. Jackson explained it all, even though the files were missing from her office. Darlene Waring had nursed along what Dr. Jackson called a 'sport,' a natural mutation of a marigold. Those pitiful plants Arnie gave you were descendants of her seeds. A year before she died, she sent seeds to Dr. Eastman. She'd heard him speak and thought he might be interested in what she'd found. He replied that the plants he'd grown with the seeds were useless. Too sprawling, unreliable colors, too fragile stems, and a bunch of other criticisms. Or words she took to be criticisms."

"But he admitted he'd grown them?" Jane asked.

"Yes, and Arnie in his own distinctive way interpreted it as a devastating insult to her that weakened her to the point that she didn't take care of herself when she became ill. He blamed Eastman for her death."

"That's unreasonable. It's why I doubted what I saw and smelled on my hands when I dropped the vase and handled the plants he'd given me."

"Not unreasonable to him. He's never accepted that she was ill simply because she had a fatal disease. We'll never know, of course, whether she was really as upset as he thought she was. But when he got his computer and started to cruise the Internet, one of the first things he looked up was any references to Dr. Stewart Eastman."

218

"That's something I hadn't thought about," Jane admitted. "I just thought he was a pretty up-to-date old guy to even have a computer."

"He found lots of references to Eastman's patents. And a piece from a plantsmen's journal hinting that Eastman was working on a marigold."

"Eastman told us nobody developing a new patent plant should ever talk to anyone but a reliable trialler."

"Apparently he hadn't taken his own good advice."

"How did Arnie come to consult with Julie Jackson?"

"She'd had a kitchen fire years ago, and being a good fireman, he went back the next day to instruct her in fire safety. He walked through her house, showing her dangers. That's how he knew her office was in the basement. He asked what she did and she explained her job. Part of it, as you suspected, was giving reports on plants to be patented. She'd worked with Eastman when he got ready to patent his marigold, so Arnie paid her to grow his seeds and compare the results."

"Which weren't favorable, I assume."

"Not at all. She told me a lot of details of the differences, most of which I don't understand, but some other expert would. Something about cell-wall structures and DNA comparisons. It must have cost Arnie a bundle for her tests. And the results showed that even if Eastman had developed his marigold from Darlene Waring's seeds, he'd spent years culling the best and raising a much superior plant, and Arnie shouldn't pursue it in court because he'd surely lose."

"Another insult to Darlene," Jane said.

"So when Arnie learned she was teaching this class, it scared him. This is only a sideline to whatever she normally does, but he thought it was the only thing she did and she might mention it in the class. He knew her house. He knew her office. He mistook her sister for her leaving that morning and thought the house was empty. He swears he was only going to filch the files, but she came out of the little bathroom in the basement and caught him at it. He swears he didn't mean to hurt her, he was only trying to get away from her with the files and she pursued him."

"And then he was angrier than ever at Eastman for putting this over on his late wife. I'll bet he blamed Eastman for making him do such an awful thing," Jane speculated.

"Almost word for word for what he said in the interview room. He'd seen pretty serious injuries in his time that the people recovered from and was afraid she'd tell Eastman about him. So he had to kill Eastman."

"How did he get Eastman out of the house?"

"He lurked in the backyard in the dark until Eastman came outside to smoke a cigar. Apparently he'd seen him do it before out in front and figured if he waited long enough, he'd catch up with him and ask about the construction of the compost heap. And the ploy worked. Eastman was a large man, but not a strong one. Arnie worked hard all his life and went to the gym every other day to keep fit after he retired. It must have been easy for him to overpower Eastman."

"This makes me so sad. I hate to think of that poor old man having to undergo a trial."

Mel took her hand and was quiet for a long moment. "He won't have to do that. He had a stroke an hour ago and died before they got him to the hospital."

Jane was shocked. "It was *my* fault."

"No, it wasn't. We'd found some fibers on Eastman's clothes and the rough wood the compost bin was made of that weren't from anything in his own wardrobe at his Chicago home or his home upstate. Nor were they from anything the housekeeper's son had. They were distinct enough to identify easily as soon as we narrowed the field of suspects. He'd have been found out eventually."

"I'm sorry I snooped this time. I wish I'd never signed up for the class or let my mind dwell on things that were none of my business."

"Murders need to be solved, Janey. No matter how the information comes about. The family and friends of victims need to know how and why it happened. It doesn't bring their loved ones back, but it helps settle their minds. And the only person in the world who contributed to Arnie's crimes was Arnie himself."

"You're just saying that to make me feel better."

"No, I'm not. It's part of what I do for a living. I understand how you feel, but you're wrong to blame yourself in any way. Arnie was very devoted to his wife, but he turned that devotion into evil acts that were entirely his own responsibility."

221

Sunday afternoon Katie made the same cake again. Mike came home about five o'clock all sweaty and dirty. "I put in some overtime today moving around a load of cow manure. I had Black Forest cake with Kipsy the other night. It was excellent, but not as good as the one Katie made. I guess I'll stick around tonight."

"No date with Kipsy?" Jane said with hope in her voice.

Mike grinned. "It's none of your business, you know. But no."

"Have you fallen out with her?"

"I never fell in with her. Dating for a couple nights was her idea and it worked like she said it would. I've got to get a shower before dinner."

Jane trailed him upstairs. "Explain!" she demanded.

He was laughing at her as he sat down on the top step. "See, Kipsy had this theory. When guys of her type, the rebellious ones, see her out with a boring, clean-cut, straight-arrow guy like me, they can't understand it and want to bring her back into the fold."

"Oh, yeah?" Jane said. Where was this leading?

"And when cheerleader types of girls see a guy like me with a freaky-looking girl, they want to save me from her. So Kipsy said. So we tried it out for a couple nights in a row. Went to places where there were both kinds of people. And it worked. I've been 'redeemed' by a gorgeous blonde and Kipsy met a biker she likes."

Jane stared at him. "That's the most cynical thing

I've ever heard. Aren't you ashamed of yourself?"

"Nope. It worked. I've got a date tomorrow with the blonde. Sandra. You'll like her. It's her natural color and everything. And she's nice and funny as well. I stink of cow manure, I've got to shower."

"I guess I'm glad the threat of Kipsy as a potential daughter-in-law has passed."

Mike got up in a swirl of cow smell and patted her head. "You worry too much, Mom. Don't touch that crutch until I'm out of the danger zone."

Center Point Publishing
600 Brooks Road • PO Box 1
Thorndike ME 04986-0001 USA

(207) 568-3717

US & Canada:
1 800 929-9108